HANGING ON

Suddenly, as I swung my body over to grab for another handhold, the wall around me collapsed. Once committed there was no way back. Rock and gravel peeled away and in one terrible, gut-wrenching instant I found myself dangling in midair, facing out away from the wall. I was suspended totally by my right arm, my hand wedged into a small crack in the rock face.

I tried to dig in, flailing back with my heels, but the hard rock had given way to a sandy, loose gravel that wouldn't allow me to gain a decent purchase. Desperately I threw my weight across my shoulder and succeeded in rolling over to a toe-in position, face flat against the wall. My grip was firm enough, but I knew it wouldn't last forever....

TRAIL HAND

A Western Story

R. W. STONE

LEISURE BOOKS

NEW YORK CITY

A LEISURE BOOK®

March 2008

Published by special arrangement with Golden West Literary Agency.

Dorchester Publishing Co., Inc.
200 Madison Avenue
New York, NY 10016

ISBN 10: 0-8439-6035-3
ISBN 13: 978-0-8439-6035-8

Printed in the United States of America.

10 9 8 7 6 5 4 3 2 1

Dedicated to the memory of Bertram A. Stone.
A kind gentleman and loving father, he taught by honorable example. Respect the rights of others, but defend against those who would deny yours.

TRAIL HAND
A Western Story

Chapter One

The boy strained hard against the powerful arms pinning him back. Although strong for his age, the thirteen-year-old was clearly no match for three adults, especially men as ruthless as these.

The youth screamed angrily, violently kicking and thrashing about as he watched the knife being drawn from its sheath. His eyes widened in terror as the cowboy thumbed the edge of his blade. He had to know it was useless to struggle, but this boy was Kiowa and the thought of quitting never occurred to him. It would be better to die fighting—at least then his spirit would live on, forever proud.

I practically rode my Morgan stallion into the ground trying to reach him, but made little if any progress. It seemed as if the very ground itself was fighting against me. Sweat flew from the bay's neck as the sun's heat combined with droplets from his nose to produce small clouds of steam.

The stallion snorted as we raced on, tugging furiously at the reins, but, strangely, the more we rode, the longer the distance we had to cover grew. It was as though time itself had stood still.

A hairy arm raised a long razor-sharp dagger, its wicked triangular blade reflecting the sun's glare. The Indian boy's chest heaved, but his

Kiowa war cry was suddenly cut short as the arm holding the knife plunged downward. The three men all laughed as his limp body fell slowly toward the ground.

My own scream caught in my throat as I bolted upright in bed, sweat dripping down my face. I shook my head clear of the dream, and, as I regained my senses, I immediately regretted having taken that *siesta*. It was one local custom I never truly learned to appreciate.

I got up, walked over to the dresser at the far end of the room, and poured some water from a large clay pitcher into its matching bowl. After washing up, I took an old rose-patterned towel off the wall hook and dried myself while staring out the window. The second-story room of the boarding house where I currently rented overlooked the town's main street, but, as usual for this time of day, there was nothing to be seen but the occasional tumbleweed.

It didn't take me long to decide on two things. One was that I was badly in need of a change of scenery. The second was that at least for now I'd settle for a stiff drink.

It was a lousy way to start the afternoon.

The sign outside read Las Tres Campanas—The Three Bells. There wasn't a bell anywhere in sight. It was just a typical *cantina* and like others common to that part of the country, small, brown, hot, and dusty. No piano players or fancy mirrors would ever be found decorating this place, although there were a few ropes and some old wine bottles hung up on the walls.

The town of San Rafael hadn't grown much in the last couple of years since it wasn't close enough to the main border crossings to attract the cattle trade. Some Texicans did occasionally drift in, but aside from a few tired and overheated local peasants, the only other regular patron of the *cantina* was a scrawny cur dog who was currently sitting in the corner chewing contentedly on the remains of a big gray rat. Dogs, I'd noticed, tend to be better ratters than most cats.

The cur had a notched right ear and, ever since a horse had stomped him, was missing half his tail. The dog smelled so badly everyone tried to give him a wide berth, but even though the room was big enough to hold more than a dozen tables, his stench was still annoying, even at the opposite end near the door. Of course that wasn't enough to stop the locals from drinking there, since the tequila served in Las Tres Campanas was the smoothest in town. The *cantina*'s owner, Felipe, also cooked the best plate of enchiladas, fríjoles, and Mexican rice anyone ever tasted.

I was leaning on the bar at the far corner, sipping mescal and trying to forget a heat that was already making rippled waves outside. I had learned to favor the drink even though I still couldn't bring myself intentionally to swallow the ever present worm that most *mejicanos* swear is the best part.

Admittedly Las Tres Campanas wasn't much when compared to other saloons I'd been in. Its bar was just a five-foot high wall of adobe with four planks laid down on top, and the wood was so poorly cut there wasn't a straight or level surface in the whole affair. There were a few lit candle stubs stuck into some old cut-out peach cans running along its length, but most of the light in the *cantina* came from a couple of hanging oil lamps that offered up more smoke and smell than actual brightness.

Two large round ceiling beams ran down to the bar top. They were meant to support the roof, but most days it seemed they were used more as targets for knife throwing practice. It was a situation that caused considerable displeasure for the bartender, a short burly sort named Ramón, who was constantly forced to duck for his life.

I had been inside the *cantina* for about an hour, minding my own business, when a conversation between two young *vaqueros* caught my ear. I wasn't intentionally eavesdropping, but what with them sitting at the nearest table I couldn't help overhearing. When they started talking about a drive west, I perked up.

My pa always said that my curiosity would get me in big trouble someday, and, as always, things would eventually prove him right. At the time, of course, I didn't know that, but, even if I had, it probably wouldn't have mattered much. If one more person in town had commented to me on how the humidity was actually worse than the heat, I would have plugged him on the spot, and in general I'm a peaceful sort. That's how bad things had gotten.

It was hot, I was bored, and the prospect of leaving this pueblo had finally gotten the better of me. While my luck hadn't completely run out, there had been better days, so by the time my drink was finished I'd already made up my mind to get out of town and back to work. I wanted to be out on the trail again, and these two *vaqueros* represented a glimmer of hope in otherwise dull circumstances.

One doesn't just butt into a conversation with strangers, especially when they're *mejicanos,* so I approached them cautiously. Their lingo might previously have presented a problem for me had I not picked up a little Spanish while hanging around the *cantina* owner's daughter, Pilar. Unfortunately she was yet another reason I was anxious to head for the far country.

Unbeknownst to her father, "Pili" and I had been seeing each other for some time, although I often suspected I wasn't the only one so honored. With her waist-length hair, sun-bronzed complexion, and full figure, Pili could attract a lot of attention, especially in a small town like San Rafael. That girl had the singular knack of making a fellow feel like he was the only man she'd ever desired, a feeling she created simply by glancing at him with a smile.

The problem was that her temper was usually as hot as her body. Seems Pili wasn't content to keep things merely on a friendly basis, and I'd temporarily forgotten what most men supposedly learn at a very early age, namely that being completely truthful is not always the best course to pursue when dealing with an armed and angry girlfriend.

In fact, the last time we saw each other I almost got my head dented by a flying skillet, an assault I was lucky to survive. But all things considered, the Spanish I'd learned from her did come in handy, and I was now fairly sure that, if need be, I could at least make myself understood.

The two *vaqueros* at the next table were drinking

beers laced with liberal amounts of freshly squeezed lemon, something the locals seem to favor doing to the suds served at Las Tres Campanas. Personally I just thought it put the finishing touches on what was already a godawful brew, preferring instead to order drinks from bottles labeled by someone other than Felipe. I had Ramón pour me another mescal before heading over to their table. My glass was still in my right hand, the intent being to appear a little less threatening.

Once, in a Kansas City stockyard, I had tipped the weighing scales at 230 pounds. Consequently, at six foot three, my size sometimes had a rather nervous effect on others in town, regardless of what I did. This time I hoped that wouldn't be the case since I was searching out work, not trouble. Even so, you never know about strangers, especially in a *cantina* south of the border. It's a wise man who never takes anything for granted.

A couple of months earlier, for example, two drunken, out-of-work Texicans decided to take out their hostilities on a black cowboy who went by the name of Sonora Mason. I guess he just happened to be drinking in the wrong place at the wrong time. The Texicans had laid in wait for him, outside, and then jumped him from behind when he rounded the corner. They dragged him into a back alley and beat him so badly he coughed blood for three days.

The locals figured that the two just felt like beating up on someone, and didn't much like blacks. I happened along shortly afterwards and heard someone moaning in the alley. What I found wasn't a pretty sight.

With his eyes swollen shut and three busted ribs, Mason wasn't in any shape to walk, so I carried him over to the doctor's office. The next day I checked in on him and helped prop him up while the doctor wrapped his chest with some wet rawhide strips that hardened into a corset-like affair. The doctor also had me fill a prescription for a yellow tea called manzanilla with *morphia* added to it for pain. Surprisingly by the third day, in spite of the doctor's warning to stay in bed for at least another week, Mason was up and around. The next morning he cut out of town early.

What those two Texicans didn't know was that Sonora Mason trailed with a band of *mejicano* outlaws. "*Muy malos*" as they say. Rumor has it his group eventually caught up with the pair, and it's been said that, when he got through revenging himself, Mason was satisfied that neither of the two would ever father any more children. Like they say, nobody takes anything for granted in a *cantina*.

Fortunately for all concerned, the two *vaqueros* acted friendly enough when I approached their table.

"*Con permiso, caballeros,*" I said in my best, although admittedly not very good, Spanish accent. "*¿Alguien habla ingles?*"

As they turned to face me, their bodies shifted subtly so as to keep their holsters free of the table. These two were obviously careful, and experienced in the ways of things.

The one to my right was a head taller than his companion, and sported a small clipped moustache. He had broad shoulders, and a wide gray sombrero that hung back on a rawhide strap. The other *vaquero* was darker, clean shaven, and slightly thinner. Although neither of them could have yet reached their twentieth birthday, both their faces were heavily weather-beaten.

As I stood waiting for a reply, I noticed their eyes drifting down toward the holster on my hip, and then back up in surprise. By now I was used to this sort of stare from others because hung on my right hip was an ivory-handled Colt Navy .36-caliber, gold-and nickel-plated, and scroll-engraved. It must have presented a strange contrast to the rest of my clothes, which in my current economic state were far from elegant. What a saddle bum like me was doing with such a fine sidearm was a story in itself.

Back home, my father ran a small but efficient ranch. While we never had an abundance of any one thing, Pa always saw to it that our family never went without the necessaries. He worked hard and led a relatively quiet life, but never talked about his life before he married Ma. Even so I always suspected that before he settled down, Pa had ridden the river a time or two. I never knew a better man with rifle or knife, and back home the folks are all good!

Some years ago the county held a fair, complete with a shooting contest that offered a pair of presentation Navy Colts as first prize. This wasn't any ordinary turkey shoot however, not with a matched brace of Colts as first prize. Actually there were several events that all had to be completed before a winner would be chosen. The bull's-eye and distance accuracy trials narrowed the field a bit, but what really thinned the ranks were the moving target competitions.

In one event a whiskey jug was hung by a rope from a tree limb and then a large wooden board with a hole cut out in its center was placed in front. The trick was to hit the swinging jug through the hole in the board from 100 yards away. Other competitions entailed shooting objects thrown in the air, targets hidden behind other objects, and shooting increasingly smaller targets.

Pa and I naturally had to try our luck. I didn't claim to be in his class, but when the finalists narrowed down to just the two of us, I could see a smile grow on his face. My old single-shot wasn't near as fine as Pa's repeater, but I had filed and shaped the stock to fit my shoulder better, and loaded my own shot.

The final contest was the hardest. This time the targets weren't moving; the shooters were. A silver dollar was placed on top of a six foot long post that had a small notch cut into it to hold the coin upright. We were required to shoot at it from twenty-five yards out. It wasn't a hard distance to make, unless you're trying the shot while cantering by on horseback.

Of course, Pa won the whole match, but not by much. I was real proud of him, although I do admit to being a touch disappointed in my own performance. As much as I loved my pa, secretly I'd wanted to best him and prove to the family that I'd finally grown up. At the time I merely wanted to earn more respect, but I know now that growing up isn't the same as being grown up. Respect isn't won quickly; it has to be earned gradually.

Truth is, although that brace of Colts was a thing of beauty, I had never really had any false hopes about keeping them, even if I had been lucky enough to win. Everyone knows small-time ranchers don't need fancy engraved shooting pieces, and it stood to reason that Pa would sell the brace for more livestock, regardless of which of us won.

Sure enough, not long after the fair ended, one of our neighbors, Jethro Hamilton, brought over some new Morgan horse crosses for our ranch. Pa had been eyeing them for quite some time, but he never had had the asking price before.

I hadn't seen the velvet-lined gun box the Colts arrived in since the contest, so under the circumstances I figured Pa had been more practical about things than I would have been if our positions had been reversed. I truly never expected to ever see those pistols again.

About a month later, on my fifteenth birthday, I was flabbergasted when Pa handed me one of those Navy Colts complete with a tooled leather holster obviously made to fit my rather substantial frame.

The present caught me totally off guard.

"I figure you really tied with me in that contest, what with havin' to use that old hand-me-down rifle of yours," Pa explained, "so I kep' the pistol you ought to have won. Swapped the other Colt, plus a good pocket watch and some grain, for the Morgans."

I knew that watch was a favorite of his, but when I started to protest, he just shook his head.

"It was a fair trade and at the same time it saved me from havin' to fret over your birthday. Besides, your ma figures, if worse comes to worst and need be, you can always sell it to he'p git yourself out of trouble." Pa smiled and continued on. "Your Uncle Zeke is the best leather worker I know, and he made this holster for your birthday, so don't ever let me catch you spoilin' it with studs an' the like. Remember, a fancy-lookin' rig with a pistol like this can get anyone in trouble." He stared at me a while as if thinking that meant *especially* someone like me. "A handgun is a serious tool, and a holster is only something for carryin' and protectin' it. Neither one is for showin' off."

I could tell he was dead serious, but there was also a hint of family pride in his eyes. It was the same pride that showed in my uncle's work. The leather belt had been carefully etched and sewn with elegant patterns to highlight the open top Slim Jim holster, designed to do justice to the pistol without being obvious.

Pa was wearing a Remington .44 Army in a worn belted holster that day, one I'd never seen before. We were standing opposite a large tree out back, when Pa reached into his pocket and brought out a silver dollar which he subsequently placed on the top of his right hand. He stood there holding his gun hand, palm down, at waist level with the dollar on top. Before I knew what happened, he'd drawn and fired, all before the coin hit the ground! I was left speechless.

"Don't be fooled by this, Son . . . a lot of shootists can beat the coin. Some use a poker chip for effect and others can do it timed in less than a second. But I'm not gonna teach you circus tricks. A person has a given right to carry a gun for protection, but when you carry, you hold a grave responsibility, to yourself and others. Remember, speed is only a small part of using a gun and won't impress those what count. They know it also takes a level head, accuracy, and no small amount of courage to face someone in a draw."

For the rest of the afternoon, and for many thereafter, Pa taught me the basics of handgunning. From what I now know about things, what was basic for Pa was downright sophisticated for most folks, and over the years I'd have more than one occasion to be grateful for all his teachings.

That's why I didn't overreact to the hard stares the men gave me that day in the *cantina*.

The *vaqueros* looked me over for a while before the taller one finally answered.

"*Sí, señor,* we speak your language. What can we do for you?"

Don't know why I was surprised that they spoke English so much better than I did Spanish, but it did make things easier, so I just pulled up a chair and relaxed into conversation as if we already knew each other a good while.

I let on right off that if there was work to be had around cattle or horses, and involved leaving town for distant parts, I was available.

The taller of the two *vaqueros,* Miguel, explained that they both worked for *Don* Enrique Hernandez de Allende, on a *hacienda* some distance to the south. They were planning to drive their horses north and then west to California, where apparently the *don*'s brother-in-law had another ranch. The other fellow, Francisco, told me they'd been sent to town for supplies and that they were preparing to return to the *hacienda* first thing in the morning.

"If you're interested in work, you will have to convince our *caporal,* the . . . ah . . . how you say it . . . ramrod? But, he realizes it will be a hard drive and we will have need of a scout who knows the country north of our border," he added encouragingly.

A few years back, not long after my seventeenth birthday, a flu epidemic took my ma, and shortly thereafter Pa died. There was no keeping me home after that, so I left the ranch to my sister Rebecca and her husband, and headed West on my own. Whatever the reason I gave at the time for leaving, the truth is I was aiming to duplicate what I imagined to be Pa's mysterious and exciting past. I rode West that spring with his rifle, an old broke-in saddle, and the pick of the Morgans, a large sable bay stallion.

That old saddle never did fit me well and was soon traded for a bigger one. Later that year, I also replaced the old rifle for a newer model Henry repeater at Freund's gun smithery in Laramie. While there I picked up a spare cylinder for my Navy .36-caliber and had their gunsmiths, two brothers named Pruitt, modify its front. The job they did building up the sight almost tripled the pistol's distance accuracy, and, by filing its sear and lightening the trigger pull, they made that Colt's action work smooth as silk.

Since that time I'd traveled a fair share, mined some, ate a lot of cattle dust, and tried to keep the trouble that always seemed to follow me around down to a minimum. I could ride most Western trails with my eyes closed, and many of the areas that I didn't explore personally had been explained to me by scouts, hunters, and trappers I'd met along the way.

I was smart enough to realize that most folks I'd meet would have something or other to offer, so I always tried to avoid a natural tendency to run on at the mouth. Even as a youngster I'd listened carefully to my elders. Some of the older men I'd met could describe places in ways not found in picture books and for the most part you could follow their words better than lines on a map. I remembered their words well.

So, with my experience, I had no trouble convincing the two *mejicanos* that they wouldn't find a better scout, and they agreed to introduce me to *Señor* Hernandez. Of course, the extra round of drinks I sprung for helped some, and early the next morning we left town together, heading south. I still rode the Morgan bay. After all we'd been through I wasn't about to trade him.

Chapter Two

During the ride out to the *hacienda* I had a chance to get to know the other two a little better. Miguel and Francisco like most *vaqueros* were of Mexican-Indian extraction. Francisco was from Jalisco, which was somewhere farther west, while Miguel was local. They'd been riding for *Señor* Hernandez for over five years, and seemed to be better off than most cowpokes I'd known.

Although I'd found *vaqueros* to be just as good on horseback as any northern wrangler, their horses always seem smaller, thinner, and more loose-coupled than the Texas cutting horse tends to be. These two *mejicanos,* however, rode a dapple gray with a white star and stripe and a well-muscled strawberry roan that would look good anywhere. We were also leading four strong pack mules that had no problem carrying a rather heavy load of supplies. *Señor* Hernandez apparently took very good care of his men, and obviously appreciated quality livestock.

Once we got out on the trail Miguel's mood began to change; he wasn't as talkative as he had been in town for one thing. I knew he was hung over a mite, but it was more than that. He seemed to be sulking about something. For a man just leaving town that usually meant girl trouble, but Francisco didn't know who, and I wasn't about to ask.

We decided to leave Miguel alone until he was in a better mood, and meanwhile Francisco and I began to swap war stories. Francisco had grown up an orphan in a monastery whose monks were grooming him for the religious life, and it was there he learned both English and Latin. In fact, were it not for his having been sent to town on his thirteenth birthday, he'd probably be Father Francisco by now. It seems that he had been helping to load the mission's wagon out in front of a general store, when a *vaquero* rode up and asked Francisco to tend his horse while he went inside to buy some supplies.

"I always liked animals," he told me, "but at the mission we had only a few old cows and a burro or two. Then this man come with his own horse that was, I thought, very big and . . . uh . . . beautiful. The *vaquero* was *Indio* like me, but, even so, he had this great big saddle and wore brand new clothes. When he came out of the store, he even tossed me some candy, and gave me *cincuenta centavos* for watching his horse. That was more money than I ever had all to myself." Francisco paused to swat a blood-sucking tick off his horse's neck before he continued on with his story.

"After that, everything in the Misión de la Virgen was to me very dull, and I soon became . . . you know, *aburrido*."

"Bored?" I asked.

"*Sí,* that's it. Two weeks later I sneaked out with just the clothes on my back, and walked to the *mercado* in the town plaza. I found *Señor* Hernandez there with his men and begged him for work. He was about to have one of them take me back to the mission, but when that one touched me, I punched him in the stomach." Francisco laughed. "He was much bigger than I, but it knocked his wind out."

"And you still got the job?" I asked, stating the obvious.

"*Señor* Hernandez pretended to be very mad with me at first, but then he started laughing. He said while I would probably make a poor *vaquero,* I would surely be worse as a priest. I have been with him ever since." Francisco grinned and added. "And after knowing the women, I think he was right."

I grinned, nodding in agreement as we rode along.

That night we camped near some cottonwoods and settled down to supper and the usual fireside coffee. Miguel seemed to be in a better mood.

"Miguel, you learn your English in a mission, too?" I asked.

"No," he replied. "I learned it in Tejas and Colorado."

"Really? Worked up there, did you?"

"*Sí*. About four years ago. *Señor* Hernandez often trades with a Meester Boocanon. . . ."

"The same Buchannon who owns the Double Deuce spread?" I interrupted.

"*Sí,* that's the one. You know him?"

"Only by reputation."

"*Bueno*. I was asked by *Don* Enrique to ride with the Double Dooze for six months while they moved stock north. They were short some men, so *Don* Enrique loaned me to them, as a *vaquero*."

Miguel got up and removed a short sword from

a leather sheath that was tied to the side of his saddle and began to cut some firewood. I'd noticed that nearly all the *vaqueros* carried one.

"Always figured those swords were a bit too cumbersome. Seems to me they'd get in the way," I said, my curiosity showing again.

Miguel shook his head. "The machete is really very practical. We use it for cutting firewood, and for chopping heavy underbrush. It is also good against snakes . . . when you do not wish to make noise or cannot shoot and"—he waved the sharp blade under my chin—"it can be a very deadly weapon."

"I see what you mean," I said uncomfortably.

Miguel smiled and tossed a pile of wood on the fire while Francisco broke out the coffee and beans.

"Even so, I think I'll just stick with this," I said, patting my Colt fondly.

It wasn't long before Francisco asked the inevitable questions about the Navy pistol. After I told him about my pa, he slowly took out his revolver and offered it over. It was a small .38 Smith & Wesson revolver with a spur trigger and bobbed hammer.

The finish was worn and the wood grips slightly cracked, but the barrel rifling was still good. It was clean and well-oiled. Had there been anything other than friendly curiosity about my firearm I would have known it by now, so I didn't mind letting him examine the Colt.

"If you don't mind the question . . . you have had to use this before?" he asked innocently. "I mean in a battle?"

I nodded, but didn't answer him aloud.

"Miguel is very fast, but I myself have never had to draw on another," he said, turning the Colt over in his hands.

"Let's hope it stays that way, *compadre,* 'cause it's true what they say. No one ever really wins in a gunfight."

I left it at that as we returned our pistols to their rightful holsters. We sacked out a short time later, after first checking on the horses. Before falling asleep, I pondered Francisco's last question, remembering the first time I was forced to draw in anger.

Shortly after leaving home I rode through a small town called Bensonville, on the way to Abilene. There was a saloon that caught my eye, called the Rusty Nail. I tethered my horse, went in, and ambled up to the bar peaceably. After all I'd ridden, I was dog tired, and hadn't figured on drawing any attention, but before I'd even finished my first beer, I was braced by an older cowboy sporting a brown leather vest, stovepipe chaps, and a holster worn low on his hip, Texas style. From his actions it was obvious that he was mean drunk.

"Well, lookee here, boys. Junior got all dressed up to go drinking with the men. Say, how about this?" he added, noticing my gun. "What's an overgrown kid like you doing with a fancy shootin' piece like that, anyway?" His breath was as loaded as his gun was.

I turned away, trying to ignore him, but he wasn't about to let it go. Pulling on my shoulder, he spun me around.

"Don't turn your back on me when I'm talkin', you miserable pup."

Things were souring a little too quickly. I looked around anxiously for some help, but there was no sign of a sheriff, and nobody in the place looked even the least bit concerned. In fact, the rest of the men actually seemed to be enjoying the show.

"Look, mister, I ain't looking for trouble, so, if it's all the same with you, I'll just be leaving."

When he blocked my way I realized that mine clearly had been the wrong approach. He was playing the bully, and all I'd succeeded in doing was to convince him that he could get away with it. Drunk as that cowpoke was, I wasn't about to change his mind.

"Afore you leave here, just hand over that hog-leg to someone who can put it to good use," he said, slamming his beer mug down on the bar top. He wasn't leaving me an out, but at least I had been careful enough to make sure my back was covered by a corner post.

Although I had no way of knowing if his friends would back him in a shoot-out, it appeared that, for now, he was the only serious threat I'd have to deal with. The rest seemed content just to watch the fun. He wasn't very bright and I figured his drinking might give me an edge, so I stood my ground, and quietly stared back at him.

"Come on, kid, what'll it be? Iffen you're not gonna hand that gun over, you better go for it, 'cause I don't aim to let you leave here with it. A fancy Colt like that ought to go real nice on my hip."

I thought he talked too much and was still hoping to get away without having to kill him. Looking over to the bartender, I nodded back over at the cowboy.

"Barkeep, if I shoot someone so stupid he forgets to remove the holster thong from his pistol hammer before a draw, you reckon it would be held against me?" I could clearly see his pistol actually was untied, but hoped he might not be so sure. I was counting on the effect of all that booze.

Sure enough, the cowboy glanced down to his hip, giving me all the time I needed. When he looked back up, my Navy Colt was leveled at him, its barrel pointing right between his eyes.

"Be thankful you're still alive mister," I said angrily. "I'm not looking for any more trouble, so just put your arms up and leave 'em there." I backed sideways out of the saloon, keeping the rest in sight, and quickly headed to my horse.

I was young and inexperienced, and naïvely thought that had ended things, so I didn't pay much attention to the taunting laughter that grew from the saloon as I mounted up. My gun was now holstered and I was turning to ride away when a shot rang out from behind, and a bullet grazed my vest. I whirled the bay, drew, and fired. Before I knew what had happened, I'd emptied five rounds into his chest.

It was over in an instant. I had killed a man. He was a drunkard who had shot at me while my back was to him, but I felt bad nevertheless. In the years since that time I've often wondered if a smarter man would have handled things differently.

At the time nobody questioned my innocence, but, although I rode out of town without looking back, I knew that I'd lost something there in the street. What was left of my youth died with that drunken cowpoke.

The fire burned low and an owl hooted nearby, returning me to the present. Francisco and Miguel were already snoring, so I pulled my blanket up over my neck and rolled over. It wasn't the first time I'd fall asleep reliving that shoot-out, but, as always, I hoped it would be the last.

Chapter Three

The next morning the three of us rose early and, after a quick breakfast, rode on south. We made good time over the next few days, and, when we finally crested the hills overlooking the *hacienda,* I could see for myself why the Hernandez outfit was able to raise such fine stock.

Nestled deep in a small valley was a stretch of lush grass pasture spreading out in all directions, and a river that curved along the eastern and northern borders of the ranch. That type of situation is rare for a country that tends more toward mesquite, chaparral, and dry barren stretches.

Don Enrique had settled the only fertile terrain in the surrounding area, and had managed it well. More importantly, though, in order to run a ranch this big, he had to have held it through the years against all comers. In those days a man called his own only what he was able to defend, and, as we rode in, I pondered the fact that *Don* Enrique had defended much. He would likely be a powerful man to contend with.

Once through the *hacienda*'s gate, my first impression was that things were being run efficiently. I noticed right off that the fences around the remuda were in good shape, solid and well-built. There's always work to be done on a ranch, and, judging from the condition of the grounds around the stable, it was obvious that none of the Hernandez *vaqueros* was allowed to loaf for very long.

When we tied up our horses in front of the nearest corral, I noticed an *amansador* breaking in some new horses. Up north they call wranglers who earn their pay saddle-breaking raw broncos "peelers". Miguel claimed that down here the *vaqueros* who worked as *amansadores* passed down their knowledge about bronco busting from one generation to the next. Whether true or not, it was clear this *mejicano* knew his job as well as any peeler I'd ever seen.

Some believe in taming a mustang by repeatedly throwing it down with their rope until it's dazed, and then riding it hard with spurs and quirts until it's exhausted. It's a quick but hard technique, one my pa never favored. Although this particular *amansador* sported the usual high, spiked Mexican rowels, and carried a short leather quirt, I was glad to see them rarely used, and then only to stop the bucking from getting out of hand.

The other *vaqueros* working with him were a well-coordinated team. I noticed one of them throwing what northern wranglers call a hoolihan loop—twirling the lariat onto the horse's neck from the ground up. It usually works better than an overhead throw, which can often spook a horse.

A *hacienda* is like a small community and its owner is frequently viewed by the *rancheros* who live there as almost a father figure, be that good or bad. Rather than troubling himself with the routine work involved in running a ranch, the *hacendado* usually delegates authority to a *caporal* who in turn is responsible for supervising the *rancheros* and *vaqueros* in their day-to-day chores.

This outfit was run by a *caporal*, named Chavez, who took his job very seriously. It was obvious, right off, that he wasn't half as personable as the other *vaqueros* I'd met so far. In fact, he didn't even bother to dismount when I was introduced. At first I took no offense, figuring that was just in keeping with his position. Although most *vaqueros* love to ride, a *caporal* practically lives in the saddle. After a while, riding, instead of walking, becomes a matter of pride.

Chavez sat astride a large sorrel gelding and stared down at me. He looked me over like someone being sold a lame mule, and not particularly happy about it to boot. He was not a very tall man, was dark-complected, and sported an oversize moustache. His left hand carried a long bullwhip, and the obvious size of his forearms suggested that he would be very proficient with it.

He also wore a utility knife sheathed in a garter strap tied halfway up his leather leggings. Almost all the men did, but I suspected the difference would be in his ability to use it for things other than cutting rope. Chavez had a large scar running straight down the left side of his face, which he tried to conceal by wearing a wide flat sombrero with the brim cocked down at a slant.

Before we arrived, Miguel had mentioned that his *caporal* got that scar preventing a robbery attempt in town, taking a knife meant for *Don* Enrique. The man obviously rode for the brand in the Western sense, which was something I could appreciate, so I stood quietly next to Miguel as Francisco introduced me.

After looking me over, Chavez turned to Francisco and rattled off something in Spanish a little too fast for me to catch. Most of the nearby hands began to chuckle.

"He says pretty men with fancy guns belong in carnivals, not on working ranches," Francisco explained.

It was fairly obvious that his taunting me was some sort of test, a way to size me up.

I'll be the first to admit that my sandy-colored hair highlighted what some considered rather boyish features, even for my size. The fact that, before riding into the *hacienda,* I'd changed into my favorite shirt probably didn't help much, either. I wore it for comfort and practicality, but it was an elaborately stitched mountain-style fringed buckskin, and may have looked out of place. Since some of the men were still laughing, I figured something needed to be said if a *yanqui* like me was ever to get any respect.

I knew it wasn't smart to fly off at an outfit's ramrod, but I could tolerate some things only up to a point. I stared straight back at Chavez.

"Miguel, tell the *caporal* he shouldn't judge a man by how nice his face looks," I said in a firm voice, an obvious reference to his scar.

Francisco stood quietly off to the side, looking at us in total disbelief.

Miguel looked even more uncomfortable at having been chosen to translate what I'd just said, but it was nothing compared to the look I got from Chavez. I continued on anyway, trying to remain expressionless.

"Miguel, tell him I know most all the routes north and west from here by heart, and I know where you're headed. At this time of the year, if he doesn't know where exactly the water is, he'll need someone like me along. One last thing . . . tell him that, if a brand treats its men fair enough, I'll give it as much or more as the next man."

The *caporal* seemed to chew on things a while before replying to me in broken English.

"We shall see, *gringo,* and soon I think." Before he could say any more, however, a tall gray-haired man approached us from behind. By the way the men reacted I knew right away he had to be *Don* Enrique Hernandez de Allende. Certain men almost immediately command respect by their mere presence. *Señor* Hernandez was clearly one of them.

Some Americans are always riding the *mejicanos* hard, especially those new to the Southwest, but I always found it an attitude hard to understand. I never expected any more or any less from others than what I was willing to give first. Most of the *mejicanos* I'd met seemed decent folk and many of their *vaqueros* were actually a far sight better ropers than some cowboys I know. In fact, I've seen *vaqueros* use the eighty- to 100-foot lassos like they were an extension of their own arms.

I always figured deep down most of us were pretty much alike, but while it's a cinch I don't descend from nobility, *Don* Enrique sure must have. He stood almost eye to eye with me, even at my six foot three. His back was ramrod straight, and, although he was in his sixties, I didn't see one ounce of fat on his body. He wore a large gray sugarloaf sombrero, an embroidered jacket, and a red waist sash.

There were solid silver conchos running down the sides of his velveteen pants that were probably worth more than I would earn in a year. Somehow, though, they didn't look flashy on him, but were rather more like something he'd earned. The *don*'s eyes were steel gray, and it was a sure bet they noticed everything that went on around him.

In spite of *Don* Enrique's commanding presence, it was hard for me to pay much attention to anything other than the sight beside him. The woman standing off to his left was truly a vision. Dark black hair, green eyes, and a fair complexion would stir any man under the right circumstances, but this was different.

Señorita Hernandez was about the most beautiful woman I had ever seen, real life and pictures included. Her eyes seemed to stare right through a man. She stood by her father's side, wearing a black skirt and a *charra*-style blouse that highlighted a figure women would fight over, and men would gladly die for.

They say that cowboys pride their hats so much they dress from the top down and undress from the bottom up. Maybe so, but that afternoon my flat brim flew off into my hands with a sweep that would have made my ma proud.

"Mucho gusto," I said, offering her my best smile.

Before she could reply, *Don* Enrique abruptly spoke out. "My daughter Rosa María and I both speak your language, *señor*." He was polite, but still the tone was there, as if cautioning me about his daughter and reminding me I was still a stranger.

I caught his drift and simply nodded back at him.

He turned to listen to his *caporal*, who strategically placed himself between the two of us before replying. I caught enough to understand Chavez was explaining who I was and how I was looking for a riding job. What I couldn't figure out was whether he was giving me the benefit of the doubt, or ending things before I even got half a chance.

Meanwhile, I was content just to exchange smiles with the *señorita*. I had time to reconsider the *caporal*'s joke about pretty men, but, right then and there, I was glad to have inherited my pa's looks. I only hoped the *señorita* was, too.

"My men know every part of Méjico from here to Chiapas, *joven*, but few have traveled much in what is now your country."

My concentration reluctantly shifted back as *Don* Enrique addressed me directly.

"Of late we have little reason to trust your countrymen, but Francisco and Miguel both speak well of you. We plan to leave here within the week, so, if you still wish to hire on, you may join the *vaqueros* in the bunkhouse." He gestured to a long building off to the far right.

"Thank you, sir, I will," I replied. "But since I wasn't sure of the if or the when of the job, I'll just stay the night. First thing in the morning I'll head back to town. Left some things that'll need tending to first," I explained. "Then, if it's all right with you, I'll join the drive when you cross over, just north past town."

"*Muy bien,* as you wish, *joven.*"

Don Enrique seemed satisfied, but I could tell Chavez was far from pleased. That was understandable. A ranch foreman likes to know more about the men he rides with than what I'd offered Chavez, but I hoped he'd cool off once we hit the trail and began working together. In the meantime, I tried my best to connect with Rosa without appearing overly attentive. Riding away without getting better acquainted with her would be hard for me, but there was little I could do other than hope to leave her with a good first impression.

After I put my horse up, one of the ranch hands, a short stocky lad named Rogelio, showed me to the bunkhouse. Buildings on the *hacienda* were constructed a little differently from those on northern ranches. Up north they tend toward sod roofs and dirt-floored houses, with walls made from logs chinked with clay. The cracks are usually patched with leftover newspaper and the shacks heated with iron stoves.

Down here things were much different. Both the bunk and chuck houses were long, one level, tile-roofed affairs. Their adobe walls were cemented with mud about four to five feet thick, which tends to keep things cooler in summer. There weren't any indoor stoves here, either, since it was usually much too hot. Instead, the cooking was done in clay ovens, or *hornos,* kept just outside the buildings.

The *hacienda* supported a lot of women *sirvientas,* who were kept busy washing, sewing, and tending to their young. Out in front of the bunkhouse sat an old *ranchero* who had to be ninety if he was a day. During the whole time I spent on the *hacienda* he just sat there on a cut-out keg, quietly watching the others and smoking the remnants of a cigarette whose ashes kept falling into his lap. From the size of that pile of ashes I'd say he smoked quite a few during the day.

I didn't really expect any fancy lodgings, but the evening spent in the bunkhouse was surprisingly comfortable. Living in another territory can be unsettling enough, but on top of that I was starting work with strangers who all spoke a foreign tongue. If it weren't for the *vaqueros'* sense of humor and Miguel's help with the translating, I would have been completely lost.

Rogelio directed me to a slat cot in the far corner, and then shoved a wooden tack box next to it to store my kit. He then pointed out various aspects of the *hacienda* and introduced me to a few of the other hands. Miguel and Francisco still had to unload the supplies we'd brought, but, since I felt out of place just standing around, I decided to lend them a hand.

Unloading four pack mules and storing supplies wasn't all that hard, but it did cause me to work up quite an appetite. When combined with a full afternoon's work, the smell from those *hornos* helped remind me it was near dinnertime and, judging from the growling sounds emanating from Miguel's stomach, it was plain I wasn't the only hungry one.

As soon as the last box of nails and spools of wire were stored, we hurried back, anxious to get first crack at the chow. Even taking my hunger into account, the chuck house meal was still real tasty, with lots of refried fríjoles, big soft tortillas, and cheese mixed in.

Mejicanos favor lots of jalapeño chile peppers and pile them high on everything. I've always been one willing to follow local customs, but this time I carefully avoided the jalapeños, remembering a whole day on horseback spent nursing the burning effects of those hot peppers on my poor *gringo* stomach. I wasn't anxious to repeat it.

After dinner the *vaqueros* settled down to the usual bunkhouse chores. Some cleaned tack, a few played cards, one told tall stories, and another played the inevitable *guitarra*. I decided to walk off dinner and took a stroll around the *hacienda*.

The Hernandez main house was situated right where the river curved and the water had a pleasant cooling effect. But more importantly, having a river wrap around behind the house as it did served as a natural barrier against unwanted or unexpected visitors. I reasoned that it would make the house an easy place to defend, in case of attack.

I felt no need to sneak around, but over the years I'd developed a tendency to position myself in shadows, or with my back to something solid, a habit that has saved my hide on a number of occasions while alone on the trail. I soon found myself standing under a nearby tree, admiring the layout of the house when *Señorita* Rosa suddenly appeared on the verandah. She stood there silently looking up at the evening sky, occasionally running her fingers through her long silky hair.

I watched silently for a while before finally speaking out. Apparently she hadn't noticed me.

"*Buenas tardes, señorita,*" I said softly while slowly emerging from under the tree so as not to startle her. Evidently it didn't work, for she gasped rather loudly.

"Didn't mean to frighten you," I said apologetically. "I was just admiring the *hacienda* when you came outside."

"It is all right," she replied in English. "You took me somewhat by surprise, although I have to admit that is usually not easy to do to me. I have lived on the trail many times with my father and try to notice such things."

"You should be very proud of him," I replied. "This is one of the most pleasant places I have been to in quite a long while."

"*Sí,* I am very proud." She nodded. "It has been very hard for Papa. My mother died when I was born and he was forced to raise me alone."

"I lost my folks a while back, too. I'm sorry."

Rosa came closer to the railing at the end of the verandah as we continued to converse. She explained why the drive was so important to her family. *Don* Enrique's only other living relative, a younger sister named Ana, had married an American, apparently an ex-military man, and had moved to California with him. The two of them were now struggling to build up a new ranch from scratch. Unfortunately Rosa's aunt had written that of late land grabbers were trying to force them out and steal their ranch.

"California was once our land," Rosa said bitterly. "Now they treat *californianos* and *mejicanos* like they somehow don't belong."

Sadly I couldn't disagree with her.

"Fortunately for us, though, horses are badly needed right now in that whole area. The economic success their sale will bring should allow my uncle to fight the others off," Rosa added. "But, meanwhile, *mi tía* says they are just barely getting by."

"If you don't mind my asking . . . why doesn't your pa just send them the money?" I inquired. "With a big *hacienda* like this he should be doing well enough to afford it."

"My father has a lot . . . uh . . . *como se llama* . . . tied up in livestock, and he has spent much trying to develop new line crosses. Also, *mi tío* is a very proud man. He simply would not take charity, even from family. So it was my idea to let my uncle sell our horses in his part of California, where the prices are higher, and then split the money with my father. That way they both will profit. But, you see, our problem will be the difficulty of taking so many horses such a distance through your country." After a brief pause she added: "That is why my father needs a good scout. I do hope you will be of help."

I couldn't possibly say no to those eyes, or to her smile, and quickly assured her I would do my best.

We continued to talk for a short time longer. Rosa always stayed in the light on her side of the railing as was only proper for a *señorita* in her situation. I could tell that the more we talked, the more uncomfortable she became, perhaps fearing her father might intrude, or think it improper for her to be alone with a man so long.

As for me, I could easily have stayed there all night listening to the sound of her voice, but after a while I began to have a rather strange feeling. It was sort of like having someone staring at the back of my head. It first started after I heard some leaves rustle behind us. Although I couldn't see anything out of the ordinary, I was still bothered by a strange something I just couldn't explain.

If someone was prowling around out there, I didn't want the *señorita* involved. Besides, a fellow ought to know how to court a woman without overstaying his welcome, so I soon bid her a good night, repeating my promise to do my best.

I returned to the bunkhouse by a different path and noticed nothing unusual. Even so, I have a sixth sense about some things, one I've grown to trust. I couldn't shake the uncomfortable feeling that we had been watched.

The next morning found me up early. It was already so hot I worked up a sweat just currycombing my horse and picking out his hoofs. I'd thrown my saddle on the bay and was in the process of cinching it up when I felt a strong tap on my back. I turned to find the *caporal* almost flat against my face, looking madder than a rabid dog.

Vaqueros usually wear large spurs with long spiked rowels that are individually designed. They are much larger than the Texican kind and somewhat awkward to walk in, so *vaqueros* often remove them when afoot. This time the *caporal* wasn't mounted. Chavez had come up on me quietly and without his spurs, so I knew something was definitely wrong.

"Hear me good, *gringo*. You do not go near the *Señorita* Rosa. You do not talk to the *señorita*. You do not even think of her! *¿Me comprendes, gringo?"*

His tone made it instantly clear that it had been either him or one of his men who had been watching us last night. It was also plain that he was either very jealous or dangerously overprotective. Either way he was in one foul mood.

"You don't even know me," I answered defensively. "Besides, don't you think it's a little early for this sort of thing?" I was trying to buy enough time to distance myself a little from him. "And, anyhow, isn't what I say and do around the *señorita* her business, not yours?" I added more firmly.

That last one was definitely the wrong question to ask at the time. After all, I was a stranger, a trail hand, and a *gringo* to boot.

Not surprisingly Chavez reacted quickly and angrily. Even though I was sort of expecting it, Chavez threw his punch so fast it still caught me off guard. If I hadn't been backing up, those fists of his would have had me out for the count. As it was, I only partially slipped a punch that clipped me hard on the ear and caught part of my cheek. After hearing bells for a second, I knew this wasn't going to be easy.

Although I can throw a fair punch myself, I've always preferred to use my size advantage by wrestling whenever possible. Rather than slugging things out and breaking knuckles on someone's face, I've found that most men don't fight well once down on the ground. Furthermore, I'd left my holster hanging on my saddle horn while Chavez on the other hand was still armed.

I took a few punches that, for the most part, I managed to block with my shoulders, and then appeared to stagger forward, setting myself up for his roundhouse right. Just as I'd counted on, Chavez swung hard, but I dropped down unexpectedly, slipped under his punch into a crouch, and shoved forward.

Caught full force in the gut with my shoulder, Chavez lost his wind. I grabbed him with both arms and spun him around as he fell. He hit the ground and rolled quickly back up, only this time without the revolver I'd snatched up out of his holster.

The *caporal* hesitated and glared at me, unsure of how best to proceed. I was mad enough to want things to continue, but only now on my terms. Without taking my eyes off of him, I unloaded the cylinder onto the ground and tossed his pistol into a nearby barrel. Then I raised both my hands up with a come-and-get-it gesture.

He spit and rushed straight at me, full force. As he bore down on me, I turned just slightly and dropped to my left knee, with my left hand high and my right low.

Unable to stop, Chavez fell onto my back, and I sent him cartwheeling over my shoulders, feet high, and flat onto his back. It would have been enough to knock the average man out, but it only winded him a little. Before he recovered, however, we heard a loud shout from behind us.

"¡Hombre! ¿Que pasa aqui?" Don Enrique was just rounding the corner when he'd called out.

Pulling Chavez up by one arm, I proceeded to dust him off.

"Sorry about that horse of mine, *caporal,"* I added quickly. "He always did have a nasty habit of kicking out like that. Hell, he's even knocked me down on occasion."

Chavez caught on quickly. He may have been many things, but a fool was not one of them. He couldn't let on to his boss what had really happened between us without getting himself in trouble for spying on Rosa, or for fighting over it.

"That horse is a devil," he said, staring straight at me. "I never even seen it coming."

"I was just leaving, *Señor* Hernandez," I explained. "When the *caporal* came to see me off, he moved a little too close to my Morgan. The stallion bucked me off and kicked out at him." I could see that *Don* Enrique was puzzled, but, since no one ventured to say any different, he had to accept it as so. "I assure you, *señor,* it won't happen again," I said while mounting up. "*Con su permiso,* I will see you in a few days," I added.

As I rode out, I could see Chavez recovering his pistol from the barrel, so I made very sure not to ride in a straight line.

Chapter Four

By the time the herd reached the border, my accounts in town were all settled. I stocked up on ammunition and said a quick good bye to Pili, who was surprisingly civil about the whole thing. Civil for her that is. She did scream something in Spanish about my *gringo* ancestry, and then indicated that I was a fool who didn't know a good thing when he saw it. She also made it clear that from that point on I could forget about any more personal attention from her. At least this time I didn't have to duck any flying kitchen supplies.

Truth is, nothing could have pleased me more, because ever since returning from the *hacienda,* I couldn't get Rosa off my mind. I never used to believe in love at first sight, but what I was feeling for her sure came awfully close.

I started the next day at first light, scouting north, to get the lay of the land, before swinging back to meet the camp. I wasn't at all surprised to find *Don* Enrique accompanying the drive, even at his age. He brought along about twelve riders, but had left his daughter behind in charge of the rest of the *vaqueros* working the *hacienda*.

Chavez, as expected, was already in the saddle, and along with the rest of his men was driving a herd of about 1,200 horses. I hadn't seen that many during my brief stay at the *hacienda,* but then again a wise man doesn't always show his hand, something *Señor* Hernandez obviously knew all too well. He must have divided his herd into various remudas in order to fool the other *rancheros,* and to foil any attempts at rustling.

Driving horses is a little different from working cattle, since they wander more and don't bunch up as tight as steers do. Horses also tend to form their own little social orders. When you try to move them around out of place, they often get to kicking and biting, preferring instead to move in lines of their own choosing.

While it's true that God never created a creature as ornery as a range longhorn, horses on the trail can spook or stampede just as easily as cattle, and as many men have been injured working around horses as cattle.

Longhorns can surely make a sane man jittery, but an unbroken cayuse can be just as unpredictable. That's why a pony won't go into a cavvy until it's about four, and it isn't till its sixth year that it finally calms down. Even so, no rider ever truly relaxes much around a working bronco till its about ten years old. Fortunately the men of the Hernandez outfit knew their jobs well and the drive started out fairly smoothly.

"These are as fine- lookin' horses as I've seen," I commented to Gregorio, one of the outriders.

"Tienen sangre española." He nodded, saying it was the Spanish blood mixed in.

From what I could make out with my limited Spanish, he was talking about an Andalusia strain and the effort *Don* Enrique had put into breeding them with local stock. It reminded me of how much Pa had wanted those Morgans to improve his own herd. Seems like regardless of language, true horsemen are the same all over.

Some Eastern folk might think that trailing horses is glamorous and exciting, but for the most part it's just plain hard work, and it starts early. Mornings are filled with a quick cup of coffee that varies in consistency from regular to glue, depending on the cook, and usually some biscuits that can either be eaten or used as wagon wheel stops.

Fact is, I've been on drives where the food was so bad the men wondered if the stew was made from old boots, and one time on the trail we passed a marker that read: Here lies the cook. Shot him cause he couldn't!

Fortunately for us, there was none better than our *cocinero,* Joaquin. He usually prepared something real spicy, wrapped in tortillas, and his coffee was more than passable. Of course, the Hernandez boys never let on to him just how good they thought it was. Nope, quite the contrary.

Joaquin always wore a red bandanna around his neck and was constantly wiping his sweaty forehead with it. Francisco and the other boys always kidded Joaquin by accusing him of using that bandanna to strain the coffee grounds. They often joked that, in order to get such a peculiar flavor, he must be squeezing it, sweat and all, back into the soup kettle when no one was looking.

In general, they made Joaquin bear the brunt of the camp jokes, something I always thought was dangerous to do to the man who prepares your food. Joaquin, however, played to the part, constantly raising a ruckus or complaining to a deaf-eared Chavez.

In reality, any one of the hands would have gladly given up his favorite saddle to keep him on as cook, and Joaquin worked as hard as anyone trying to prepare our meals the best he could. As for my part, I was pleased just to keep quiet and enjoy the grub, which I ate in formidable amounts.

Joaquin's chuck wagon was a covered, two-wheeled affair with four large water barrels tied to its sides. Aside from the usual assortment of pots and pans, it also carried an extra barrel of molasses. That's why, by the eighth day out, our cook was nursing a sore head.

Seems Joaquin had a habit of sleeping under his wagon at night with a few of the twenty some odd goats that trailed after him. One night the barrel leaked some of the syrup onto him while he slept. Joaquin awoke in a start, practically covered in ants, and bolted upright so fast he knocked himself out cold on the wagon axle. The goats didn't mind lapping up the molasses, though, ants and all. We found them under the wagon, licking Joaquin's head and face.

After a short breakfast the ponies chosen to be ridden that day were bridled, brushed, and their hoofs picked out. Only a fool would ride a horse before checking hoofs and tendons first. Unfortunately, lifting and holding a horse's four legs and picking out its hoofs first thing in the morning is not only hard on the back, it can be a real chore, especially if the horse isn't the kind to stand still for it. Many is the time I've had a bite taken out of my backside by a nasty bronco.

I was grateful that my Morgan bay always stood like a rock for me. Even so, he was strong, his legs heavy, and he had large hoofs for his size. He also had a nasty habit of swatting me in the face with that big tail of his every time I bent over.

Saddles also have to be maintained. Most of the never-ending tack work is done in the evenings, but every now and then a cinch breaks or a rein snaps and has to be replaced. A rider's tack is almost a part of him, and most of the outfit's *vaqueros* were very attentive about keeping things in good shape. A good horseman soon learns to be a combination leathersmith and poor man's tailor, not to mention farrier.

Anyone who has ridden his bottom raw in a ragged misfit saddle, or has had a stirrup leather break on him at the wrong time doesn't ever again get behind with his tack. Most working saddles aren't all that fancy, but they do have to be comfortable, and sturdy enough to withstand the constant pull of both rider and rope.

The extras in the kit are important, too. A torn saddle blanket thrown over a dirty burr-ridden hair coat will quickly rub a horse raw, cause fistulous withers, and leave his rider afoot. A working cayuse isn't brushed for show, it's done for his health, as well as the rider's.

A cowboy's boots are another item constantly in need of attention. In some places thorns will drive right through a boot toe if it's in poor shape and can actually cripple the rider. Texican boots have a higher heel than the flat *mejicano* kind and slant inward more, probably to keep the foot from hanging up, or from shooting through the stirrup in case of being bucked. Mexican stirrups—*tapaderos*—sort of solve that in their own way.

The *vaqueros* all had these round leather coverings on the front of their stirrups to help prevent this. I kind of liked the idea, so I asked Joaquin to help me sew on a makeshift pair of *tapadero* stirrup covers made from some spare dried-out cowhides. They weren't as good-looking as the rest's, but they sure did the job.

The herd of horses we were trailing wasn't yet shod, but those cayuses in the *vaqueros'* remuda had to be. Horseshoes protect hoofs from the rider's extra weight by keeping the animal's soles and heels up off of rough terrain. Even with shoes on, however, hoofs still have to be regularly filed free of sandcracks, and soles protected from penetrating wounds. There's an old saying—"No feet, no horse."—and, as important as that Morgan stallion was to me, I was glad we had a good smith along with us.

One of the biggest and surely fattest of our group was the *vaquero* they all called Chango. He was about thirty, bald as an egg, and, when he walked, it was with a sort of half limp, half shuffle. Without a doubt Chango had the flattest feet I ever laid eyes on. He also had a constant twitch in his left eye, and it took me a few days to figure out why.

Chango Lopez had apparently been the outfit's blacksmith for years. He was a big man, but always stood somewhat bent, having spent practically his whole life stooped over an anvil or some horse's leg. His hands were so big that a hoof seemed to disappear in them, and, given his size, it wouldn't have surprised me a bit to learn he shaped his horseshoes by bending old railroad ties, cold. In spite of his tremendous size and strength, however, Chango had good hands when it came to shaping and fitting shoe to hoof. He was never rough and took great pride in his attention to detail when pounding hoof nails.

Sometimes simply holding onto the leg of a cayuse that's being shod isn't enough, especially with a skittish mare or a mean bronco. One morning, after about a week and half out, I found Chango tying up a large and obviously cantankerous chestnut mare.

When a blacksmith can't get a horse to stand still, he'll often throw an assortment of ropes and nooses around its girth, neck, and leg. Done right it will act as a combination pulley and pressure snare. This way he can both lift the leg and at the same time, by snugging the rope, immobilize the animal.

The rope has to be pulled tight, but with Chango's arm size that shouldn't have presented much of a problem. I had been getting ready to scout ahead, but as I rode past him, I couldn't help notice he was limping even more than usual.

"*¿Que te pasa, hombre?*" I inquired, gesturing to his foot. "Is it broke?" I asked.

"*Sí, es mi pie,*" he answered, pointing first to his toes and then to a large grulla gelding that apparently had stomped his left foot the day before. It was a toss-up as to which of Chango's feet had been broken more over the years. It also explained the presence of his highly guarded pocket flask.

With the exception of some medicinal whiskey that was kept locked up in the chuck wagon, Chango Lopez was the only one on the trail *Don* Enrique allowed to drink. Although we all liked a good shot whenever possible, none of the *vaqueros* dared argue the point with the *don.* Instead, everyone simply shrugged Chango's ration off as a pain reliever we were glad not to have need of.

Chango was putting the final touches to his snugging harness and tying down the main knot when I noticed the shine on the rope he was using.

"It's new, right?" I asked with a sense of foreboding.

"*¿Sí, porque?*" he asked, looking up at me questioningly. Just then the knot slipped. As slick as it was, that new rope wouldn't hold the knot, and it practically smoked as the whole affair came unraveled. The big chestnut's hoof dropped point first, falling straight down like an axe blade. Chango took the whole weight of that mare's leg right on top of his bad foot.

"*¡Aii cabrón!*" he screamed, and I didn't blame him one bit. The whole left side of his face screwed into a grimace as he fought back the pain. As I rode away, I now understood his facial twitch, and vowed silently to myself never to take up blacksmithing for a living.

Joaquin and Chango excluded, things had gone well for the rest of us so far, and everyone quickly fell into a routine. Even the herd was behaving as well as could be expected.

All the horses were rounded up every morning and grouped tightly for the drive. Nobody rides nice and straight on a drive, but rather everyone constantly weaves back and forth, in and out, in order to keep a herd in order. Horses are spookier than cattle, and even a trail-wise cayuse will occasionally try to buck its rider. That's one reason Westerners ride their saddles deeper than Easterners do, and longer legged.

The problem Western riders face is that they

not only have to be able to work in the saddle, but also to relax. After several months of riding, a cowboy, wrangler, or *vaquero* develops a sort of round-shouldered, slouched-back, and bow-legged appearance from long hours in the saddle.

I once met a gent who rode one of those miniature English-style saddles. Sort of a small-skirted seat with a low cantle, and no fenders or pommel. It looked more dressing than anything else, kind of like a flat filled-in McClellan with small metal stirrups hanging down. It might have been real comfortable for a little girl, but at the time the bunch of us watching figured the dude riding it would last about two days on a real trail drive before his back went out on him. That is, of course, if he could stay on a Western bronco for more than a minute or two.

Western horses are different from those back East. They tend to be shorter coupled, with more muscle and rib bone than fat and finish. A good Western cayuse is bred for stamina, trail sense, and harsh climates, and a cowboy will often forgive a cantankerous horse if it's sure-footed or good with cattle. Only someone who is a rider can truly appreciate the relationship between man and horse. It's different than with a dog, or any other critter for that matter. A rider must care for and respect his mount, for their lives depend on one another.

According to whom you talk to, horses are either intelligent creatures, or the dumbest beasts on earth. For one thing they're the only animals dumb enough to drink themselves to death, and will run till they drop dead. At the same time, there isn't a gate built that a horse can't eventually open. I once saw a cayuse actually get down on all fours and crawl out from under a fence, and they aren't supposed to be able to do that.

Whether it's smart as a whip or dumb as an ox, the horse is the one animal a cowboy will give his life for and it's the same with *vaqueros* down south. Funny thing, I've known some of the toughest and meanest men to cry for a whole week after having to shoot their injured cayuse, while on the other hand some nice quiet types can put a horse down and get another as easily as changing a pair of pants. It's hard to figure.

Without a horse some parts of this country are certain death. Guess that's why, when you stop to think about it, horse thieving is a hanging offense, whereas bank robbing or cattle rustling just gets jail time, if that.

I remember hearing of one outlaw who'd almost made a clean getaway when his horse broke a leg. Since his shot had given him away, some of the men in the posse about to hang him wondered why he'd bothered to stop and shoot the horse.

"You must have known the sound of that gunshot would tip us off," they'd said. "You would have gotten clean away otherwise. That shot meant sure death, so why'd you do it?"

"Wasn't any other way to play it. Couldn't just leave him like that," was all he'd answered, but it was explanation enough.

No drive gets started until the working ponies are checked over and any problems attended to, and ours was no exception. After all, you can't herd animals from a wagon top; our ponies worked as hard as we did.

So for the next three weeks we continued our daily routine. *Don* Enrique left most decisions up to Chavez, who unfortunately hadn't yet changed his attitude toward me. He did allow me a free rein to ride where I wanted, but, since he often criticized my recommendations, I tended to report directly to *Don* Enrique whenever I could.

Early every morning I rode ahead to scout the terrain, not returning till about midday. I usually repeated the process in late afternoon, returning for dinner just after dusk. At dark, after bedding my horse down and having dinner, I'd walk the camp perimeter and check the sentries, enjoying the evening quiet and the cool night air.

Night on the trail can be a combination of pure pleasure and nervous tension. The sky might be clear and full of stars, but when trouble comes, it will usually start between dusk and dawn.

Some folks believe Indians won't attack at night, but that applies only to certain tribes, and even those that don't fight in the dark have nothing against scouting around, making plans, or picking off an isolated straggler. The same holds true of outlaws, most of whom prefer to hit and run.

The Hernandez night riders always circled the herd either talking quietly among themselves or singing, partly to calm the animals, but mostly to let their presence be known. It's good to remember not to ride up on someone unannounced on a drive, since to do so often risks a bullet through the chest.

Sometimes in the evening I'd wander a couple hundred yards out to relax under a rock ledge or cottonwood overlooking part of the camp. I tried to imagine someone stalking it from various angles, and then I'd check out any place I thought might bring trouble. It's a wise man who learns to relax whenever possible, but on the trail a scout soon learns to do so with one eye open. It's smart because, aside from Indians and rustlers, there's also wildlife to worry about, like cougars and prairie wolves.

You can't take the elements for granted, either. Even the driest areas can suddenly be hit by storms with lightning so bad it'll spook a herd or send a flash flood roaring down a newly formed gorge, taking rider and cayuse along with it. I've seen some of the flattest driest spots in the Southwest suddenly turn into a solid sea of mud during such squalls.

Unfortunately that's precisely what happened shortly after we turned west. It was mid-afternoon on a fairly level and open plain. I was scouting ahead. Armando was riding drag with Ricardo, and the rest of the men were scattered around, working the horses from their usual places.

Contrary to what some folks might believe, most herds, be they horses or cattle, are best driven at only a modest pace. The more experienced *vaqueros* usually ride point, keeping the herd on its course or veering the animals during directional changes. Swing riders work just behind them, but slightly off to the sides, and they are followed, farther on back, by flankers who try to stop the animals from straying and retrieve those that succeed. Following just behind them are drag riders, who constantly push the herd as well as dealing with any slow or injured animals.

Joaquin Gutierrez and Chango Lopez usually rode well behind the drag riders until mealtimes, at which point they drove up past the herd to set up for chow. Out of habit Joaquin would bed down every night up ahead of us, with the chuck wagon's tongue pointed forward in the direction of the next day's journey.

In that part of the country the average rainfall is only about five inches at most, so the arid, lime-heavy soil supports only sparse shortgrass. We all figured it was still too early in the season to expect much rain, but there was an unusually strong breeze blowing that day, and the bay was acting strangely.

At the time I was riding about a mile out when Francisco approached me at a gallop.

"El caporal me mando. Está preocupado," he said, indicating Chavez's growing concern over the change in the weather. "Look at that sky."

He really didn't have to warn me, though. I'd already noticed the thickening cloud cover, surprised at how suddenly everything had darkened. Within a period of only a few minutes a bright and shiny day turned an ominous gray. A freak storm was brewing, and, from the look of things, it promised to be one nasty torrent.

We turned our horses around and started cantering back to the herd when the first lightning bolt hit. Almost simultaneously the sky opened up like a busted bucket, with rain pouring down in gallons.

"Circle the herd!" I yelled, temporarily forgetting my Spanish.

"¡funtalos muchachos!" shouted Francisco al-

most simultaneously. We spurred our horses to a gallop, closing quickly with the herd, which was now headed straight toward us at a dead run.

With thunder as loud as cannon blasts spooking the herd, our whips and pistol fire didn't have much affect, so we angled toward the lead stallions, trying physically to turn them with our own mounts. Almost immediately Francisco and I were joined by Chavez and several other *vaqueros*.

The ground around us was rapidly becoming a quagmire and it was increasingly harder for our ponies to maintain their footing. Suddenly Francisco's horse slipped and stumbled, almost going down directly in front of the oncoming herd. My heart skipped a beat, dreading the inevitable, when Chavez flashed by me at a gallop.

The *caporal* practically came right out of his saddle, leaned sideways, down, and over, and grabbed Francisco's bridle with his right hand. Chavez spurred his own mount on ahead, while at the same time jerking up on Francisco's bridle in an effort to help keep the horse's head up, thus allowing it to regain its balance. It was a move that could easily have cost Chavez his own life as well. Thankfully he pulled it off, and, as Francisco regained control, we all breathed a grateful sigh.

"*¡Bravo, caporal! ¡Bien hecho! ¡Andale,* Francisco!" The men's shouts grew as the stallions out in front began to circle, and with them the rest of the herd.

I shook my head at Francisco who merely looked back at me in relief and shrugged.

We were all soaked to the bone. The downpour and subsequent stampede happened so quickly most of us didn't even have time to put on our ponchos. Water poured off our hats in streams. But at least the herd had turned and the horses were starting to calm down.

I looked over at Chavez as if to say that it had been much too close a call. We were tired, and sweating heavily in spite of the cold rain but, at the same time, were pleased at not having lost any of the horses.

Don Enrique rode toward us, his big gray gelding sliding in the mud as he reined in. "Good work, boys."

Chavez nodded to his boss, and then suddenly looked back in response to hearing someone call his name.

About fifty yards away, one of the *vaqueros* was shouting at us through the rain. *Don* Enrique finally spotted him and pointed back at young Jorge Morales, one of the boys who had been riding flank prior to the storm.

Jorge was small with rather girlish features, but he was a doer and a tryer, often compensating for his age and size by working harder than need be. Armando was engaged to Jorge's older sister, Eva, and the two *vaqueros* had grown very close of late. All of the men liked his jovial nature, and gladly shared their individual skills with him whenever time allowed.

Jorge was now sitting a ten-year-old piebald paint that he favored. The pony was very much suited to him, being short-coupled, spirited, and sure-footedly quick in a turn.

Chavez waved back at Jorge, motioning for him to ride on over to us.

"*¡Que aguacero! ¿Verdad, muchachos?*"

"What a drenching!" Jorge yelled back. He was wearing an old rifle slung across his back, and was reaching for a slicker I'd previously lent him. Shifting the rifle off his shoulder, he held it up in his left hand while at the same time turning around in his saddle to untie the slicker slung across the back of his saddle.

There was another *crash* of thunder when, for some reason, I suddenly had another one of those bad premonitions. While patting the Morgan's neck to calm him down, I glanced around anxiously. All at once lightning struck so close the bay jumped a foot sideways in fright. I quickly looked over to my right and, to my horror, saw Jorge Morales frozen in a strange bluish light.

Apparently his musket was acting like a lightning rod, or maybe it was the metal conchos he'd tacked all over his saddle. Whatever the reason, that lightning bolt hit him square on.

Instinctively Chavez threw an arm up to his face to shield himself from the flash, as *Don* Enrique exclaimed: "*¡Madre de Dios!*" All of us reacted out of shock and surprise.

Jorge sat there shaking like a rag doll, his arms flung up over his head, outstretched, the rifle still pointing upward in his left hand. His pony actually seemed to rise up onto the points of its hoofs, the hair on its mane and tail standing straight up. Several of the *vaqueros* around me gasped as the boy and his cayuse stopped shaking, and toppled over. They both landed flat on their sides, almost as one, like a statue being pushed over.

I spurred the bay and, together with Armando,

Rogelio, and Chavez, rushed to Jorge's aid. We jumped to the ground and ran only a step or two before stopping cold in our tracks. There was no use even checking him, since up close it was obvious Jorge was already dead. There were long black stripes of burnt flesh running down his neck and all across his back. His clothes were still smoking.

The pinto had similar stripes burned the length of its body, and everything smelled of singed hair. Rogelio pointed to a large hole under the horse's belly from which its guts poured out.

We stood for a while in silence, staring at Jorge's body, as the rain poured down on us. In spite of the continued flashes of lightning and accompanying thunderclaps, it seemed as though everything had suddenly grown very quiet, and everyone remained very still. I bent down slowly and, with Armando's help, pulled Jorge off his horse, and rolled him over on his back. Armando crossed himself and his tears combined with the raindrops running down his face.

Jorge's mouth was locked in an eerie expression of complete surprise. What bothered me most, however, was the strange look in his eyes. They were both still open, staring straight up at us as if searching for the answer to a question for which there was none. At least none that I knew of.

I felt a hand on my shoulder as the *caporal* stepped in between us and bent over. He ran his hand across the boy's eyes, closing them gently. The rain stopped almost simultaneously.

"We'll bury him here," *Don* Enrique said quietly.

Armando and I looked up at the rest of the men whose horses now surrounded us.

"Remove whatever he has of value to send his family," Chavez added.

"Yo me encargo de eso," Armando offered, drying his tears.

Several of the men dismounted after Joaquin brought back some shovels from his wagon. The rest turned their mounts around and returned to the herd.

A half hour later *Señor* Hernandez led a small ceremony for Jorge Morales. The men stood silently in a half circle around the grave, their sombreros in hand as the words were read. The manner in which the Morales boy died had touched each one of us, partly because of the sudden violence, but also because of its utterly random nature. While dying in a stampede or during a gunfight might be considered hazards of the line of work we'd chosen to pursue, Jorge's completely random death was a reminder that no man truly has control over his own life, only what he does with it.

Don Enrique's words were a comfort for those who believed there is a greater purpose to death than man could ever comprehend. As far as I was concerned, though, it was enough just to be grateful that he had died quickly and without much suffering. Jorge's family would have proud memories of a boy who grew quickly to manhood, and who died while doing his job well. That's as much as anyone can hope for.

As soon as the *don* finished, Chavez ordered everyone back into the saddle and moving. As always there was work to be done but it was good therapy, and over the next few days we made good time. True to form Chavez drove the herd as well as the men hard, leaving little time for sorrowful contemplation or remorse.

Chapter Five

Unfortunately, over the next few weeks, the working relationship between Chavez and myself failed to improve. I had yet to gain his trust and that was making my job increasingly difficult, especially since having come to an impasse over how best to proceed with the herd. It was my job as scout to find the safest route, but as usual I had a hard time convincing the *caporal* to listen to reason.

Chavez impressed me as a hard worker and his physical courage was beyond question, but, try as I might, I just couldn't say yes without his no, or offer a "hi" without his "bye."

Most of the men eventually accepted me well enough, and I'd become downright friendly with Miguel and Francisco, but it seemed that no amount of "yes, sirs" or "no, sirs" was ever going to change the *caporal*'s attitude toward me. Things finally came to a head one hot afternoon while trying to explain our differences to *Señor* Hernandez.

Chavez, *Don* Enrique, and I were sitting horseback about a mile and a half in front of the herd.

Don Enrique looked straight ahead while he spoke. "My *caporal* does not agree with you, *joven*."

"Well that doesn't surprise me," I said, glancing at Chavez. "It won't be the first time."

The *caporal* shifted in his saddle, his increasing anger obvious.

"We should continue as planned," he said to his *jefe*.

"Sorry to disagree, *Señor* Hernandez, but going straight on ahead wouldn't be very smart," I argued.

"And why not? The map suggests otherwise," he asked.

"Maps don't always tell you the whole story. Look, I know this area. While it's true that both the military and the stage line use this trail, so does the Brazelton gang, and about a half dozen other outlaws. Not to mention the White Mountain Apaches. You might have heard that the Indians have been quiet lately, and in actual fact they probably respect the truce a hell of a lot better than we do, but still you never know. I'm paid to worry about such things and I think there still might be a few hotheads who'd just love to raid a herd like this. But more importantly, if we follow this route relying solely on that map, you'll find the next five days to be mighty thirsty ones. Up ahead it's almost totally devoid of good water. Trust me, it's a bad stretch."

"But, as you say, the stagecoach and the Army feel it is the best way." *Señor* Hernandez was a cautious man.

"I don't trust him, *jefe*," Chavez chipped in his usual estimation of my worth.

I tried hard to ignore him. "The Army travels a hell of a lot better armed than we do. And remember, the stagecoach line doesn't have to water twelve hundred thirsty horses. A six-up stage moves a whole lot faster than our herd will and you know it."

"So what do you suggest?" *Don* Enrique asked.

"That we turn north for the next few days."

"*¿Norte? Esta loco el gringo,*" muttered Chavez. "And lose more time?" he added, glaring at me.

"Maybe we'll lose a few days, but we'll save a lot of horses. See, I know a small cañon north of here that's not on the map. It's blocked from view by some bluffs and the entrance is probably covered with overgrown brush by now. But there's plenty of water fed from an underground stream, or well, of some kind. I found it by accident a while back and even in midsummer there was more than enough water to go around. Fact is, if I'd gone straight ahead, it's not likely I'd be here talkin' to you. I'd be dead of thirst. Look, I figure we can cut back southwest from there. So don't worry. More likely than not we'll make up whatever time we lose having to detour north from here."

"I don't like it," Chavez said, wiping his hand slowly across his brow. It was evident his anger had lessened and that he was rethinking the situation. At any rate the final decision rested with *Don* Enrique.

"We will do as our scout recommends," he said after some consideration. Turning to Chavez, he added: "One should not ask for an opinion unless he is ready to follow it. We will camp here for now and then drive the remuda to this cañon."

"*Sí, señor,* as you wish."

Turning back to me, *Don* Enrique continued on. "I want you to ride out and survey the area. I do not want to send my men blindly into danger."

"You won't be sorry," I replied.

"We better not be," the *caporal* added, remaining true to form.

Later, Francisco, Miguel, and I rode out in search of the cañon I'd described to *Don* Enrique.

A few years earlier I'd been forced by circumstances to change directions or face the consequences. At the time the circumstances and the consequences just happened to be one and the same, namely a band of angry Apaches itching for a big white man to torture. I'd found myself stranded among them with an empty canteen and no way back to the last water hole. Even so I still counted myself lucky. Apaches don't usually give any warnings. Fact is, most of the time you don't even know they're around until an arrow flies by your head.

I'd spotted them at night entirely by accident, almost stumbling right into the Apache *ranchería* while trying to find a place to bed down. To this day I don't know why they didn't catch me. Maybe it's true what they say about how God protects the dumb and innocent.

At any rate, I knew those Apaches would pick up my trail come morning, so before they caught onto me, I hightailed it out of there as fast as I could, changing directions so often that even my horse was confused. And that's when I came upon the entrance to the valley. Well, actually the Morgan stallion spotted it first. He was as thirsty as I was and must have picked up on the smell of water.

At first it was hard to make out the entrance, but since the bay was tugging hard at the reins, I let him have his head and just sat back. I always trusted that horse's judgment more than that of most men I knew. As usual he didn't let me down.

Once we made it through the thickets that overgrew the entrance, the valley opened up like the petals of a flower. Stretching out for at least four and a half miles was a thick field of grass and a creek that originated from a pool situated at the base of a large rock overhang. Water spilled over from the pool and ran downhill spreading throughout the valley.

I dived down into that pool as far as I could, but never did reach bottom. An underground water-spout continually pushed crystal clear water upward, nourishing the whole pasture. It was an untouched piece of paradise.

Today I was in the mood for a little fun, so, after mentally reassuring myself of the entrance route, I challenged the two *vaqueros* to a race.

"Miguel, Francisco . . . catch me if you can!"

We galloped along almost until the very last minute at which point the Morgan veered toward the entrance to the valley. With the two *vaqueros* following my lead, the three of us raced full speed at what happened to be a solid wall of thickets.

I could see Miguel's look of confusion and the growing panic on Francisco's face. They kept expecting me to stop, or at least swerve, but I just leaped ahead, letting the Morgan have his head. When we finally reached the thickets, the two hauled back on their reins so hard Miguel's horse dug a trough in the ground, and Francisco was thrown clear off his saddle.

The Morgan and I raced through a patch we knew to be safe, jumping a trunk on the ground and running through the shrubs covering the entrance to the valley. When I called out to them, Miguel and Francisco must have thought they were hearing a voice from the great beyond. When they finally realized they weren't really hearing a ghost, after all, they let fly a stream of commentaries that I wouldn't care to hear repeated at a Sunday goin' to meetin'.

After we had a short look-see around the valley, it took us about two hours to clear the entrance of trees and branches, enough to make room for the wagons and the rest of the herd. Francisco and I hobbled our horses while Miguel tied a rope to his saddle horn, using it to help pull several trunks and other large rocks out of the way.

Back home children learn not to stick their hands anywhere without looking first, but after a couple of hours of backbreaking labor I got a little careless. While trying to get a better purchase on a branch that just wouldn't budge, I reached down under it without checking first. When Miguel's horse pulled back, the rope snapped and I tumbled backward with the branch landing smack on top of me.

I was completely pinned down when, to my horror, I discovered that I had been clearing the branches around an active rattlesnake pit. Two six footers were coiling, one close to my arm and the other near the calf muscle which had become exposed during the fall when my pant leg snagged.

Trapped under that branch I had no way to reach my gun. The boot was pulled halfway off and my leg was within inches of the serpent. I screamed for help, kicking sand as the snake rattled, preparing to strike. Try as I might, I couldn't free my arm. In fact that whole side of my body was caught tightly. Unable to move, my eyes were frozen on a pair of hideously curved fangs. I felt something fly by my face and a shot rang out.

Almost simultaneously the first rattler was cut in half by the machete Francisco had thrown, while the other snake exploded from the impact of Miguel's bullet. Thankfully Francisco had been right about Miguel; his draw was both fast, and accurate.

After they had me free of the tree and had dusted me off, I pulled the blade free and offered it back gratefully.

"You know, boys," I said, handing over the machete, "after reconsidering things, I just may get me one of these. You're right, they are kinda useful for working around snakes. *Gracias, hombres.*"

"It was nothing."

"Don't mention it, *amigo.*"

I didn't, but, as far as I was concerned from that point on, those two could call in their markers anytime and I'd see to it they were cashed.

Reassured that I was all right, Francisco rode back to the others to act as guide while Miguel and I made preparations to stake out the camp. The valley was just as I'd remembered it, well sheltered and with plenty of running water.

That evening was one of the most pleasant I can remember. The water was cool, the food good, and the weather even better. I remember how splendid the sun looked as it set that day, glowing soft orange as if the fire had gone from it. The moon was full, and shone brightly as wisps of clouds floated by. Even Chavez was in a good mood, although he'd never admit out loud that I'd been right.

After dinner several of the *vaqueros* went over to Joaquin's chuck wagon and retrieved the musical instruments they'd stashed there. In every group of *mejicanos* I'd ever known, there was always someone who played the guitar, and this bunch was no exception. In fact, most all of the men could pick a little, and soon music filled the night air, sometimes quiet and peaceful, sometimes loud and lively.

Armando grabbed Chango's arm and the two of them began prancing around. I tossed my sombrero in the ring and everyone started laughing as several others joined my half-baked hat dance.

A short while later, stretched out listening to the men sing an old *ranchero* tune, called *"El Cantador"*, I complimented Ricardo on his fancy rope work.

"I saw the loop you threw over that grulla trying to get away from you this morning. Nice job. I was sure he was going to beat it," I said in broken Spanish.

"Eduardo is really much better," Miguel translated Ricardo's words as he sat down alongside of us, holding a second plate of Joaquin's special hot rice. *"Arroz a la mejicana."*

They called their friend over to join us.

"Oye, Eduardo, *ven acá y trae tu reata."*

Eduardo came over, adjusting the knot on what had to be the longest lariat I'd ever seen.

"*¡Andale,* Eduardo!" shouted Armando joining in the fun. "Show the *gringo* how it's really done."

I have to admit I was impressed. Over the next

ten minutes Eduardo made that rope dance a series of *pasos* that were a wonder to behold.

Later that night, while pouring myself another cup of coffee I noticed *Señor* Hernandez sitting off to one side, alone, with an empty cup in his hand. Rather than waiting for him to get up, I took the pot over and refilled his cup.

"Mind if I sit here with you a spell?" I said in Spanish, or so I thought.

"'*Sentarme un rato*' means sit a while," the *don* replied. "But you just asked me if you could '*sentarme con una rata*' which translates as 'may I sit with a rat?' However," he said with a grin, "the answer is yes, but only if we speak English. My ears are getting too old to suffer the agony of a beginner's accent."

I laughed in agreement, but, however bad my accent might sound, I was intent on improving it, as well as my vocabulary.

"I don't stay a beginner long at most things I set my mind to," I said proudly.

"*Muy bien*. I think you will find Castellano, our original Spanish, to be a rich and descriptive tongue. One that is, in fact, even more logical than your own language."

"How's that?" I asked defensively.

"For one thing, the English always put their descriptions before the object of conversation. In Spanish we say . . . '*la casa blanca, cuadrada y grande,*' . . . or 'the house that is white, square, and large.' However, in English, you start out, instead, by describing something that has not yet been identified . . . the big, square, white . . ."—he paused—"house. You see, it is backward."

"Well, you might have a point. I never thought

about it like that," I said, pondering the idea. "But then, on the other hand, I never had any problems understanding English, and I've been speaking it since I was a kid." It was a lame joke at best.

"Of course." He smiled. "But even you will have to admit, it makes more sense to put the noun before the description. Makes the language more sensible and easier to learn."

"If you don't mind my asking," I said, anxious to change the subject, "how did someone like you, someone so learned, choose to settle in these parts? Seems like you'd have been more comfortable in the city."

"My family originates from Sevilla, in Spain. There it is the custom for the inheritance to go to the older son. My father was the best horseman in the region and was well educated in both breeding and ranch management. Unfortunately he was the second son. So you see my uncle inherited all the family lands. It seems that with our people one either works the land, joins the army, or becomes a priest, and my father was not the sort to spend his life in a church."

"So he joined the army."

"*Sí.* He was a captain with the mounted Lancers. Eventually he came to Méjico and married. As a boy I remember how he read with disgust the letters from home, and the discussions with my mother about how my uncle was ruining the land and mismanaging things. I vowed someday to create another *hacienda*, one where my father could finish his days doing what he most loved, raising fine horses.

"I have been blessed with many things during

my life, not the least of which was Rosa's mother. My beloved wife Gloria worked, struggled, and fought by my side, year after year, until we finally established a fine ranch, one my father could be proud of. One that would bring honor to our name. I even imported horses from Andalusia, the finest in the world."

"I won't argue that point with you, *Don* Enrique."

"Gracias."

"And then he joined you, your father? He helped you finish breeding this herd?" I asked.

"Unfortunately no. Papa died the very same month that the horses arrived. It was not a good time for us. My wife also died that year, soon after giving birth to Rosita."

"I'm sorry. I know how much it hurts to lose one's family."

"Were it not for Rosa María, I might have given it all up, but having a daughter to care for gave me instead more determination. I wanted to leave her something important. Wealth and power are important, *sí,* but they are not everything. I also wanted Rosa to have a sense of honor and pride, and a sense of obligation to others."

"If you'll allow me, sir, from what little I know of her, I think it's safe to say you succeeded at that."

Don Enrique smiled and nodded. "Rosa has worked the *hacienda* alongside of me all her life, and I am proud to say the *vaqueros* respect her as much as they would any man."

"Well, Chavez for one sure seems awfully protective of her," I added, remembering the clout he'd given me. "Mind if I ask you if there's anything between the two of them? You know . . . romantically?"

"*¿El caporal y Rosa?* No. They are more like brother and sister. Chavez's father worked for me as my first *caporal,* and the two children grew up together. I am not sure who fell off more horses or who had more black eyes as a child," he said, laughing, "but I do remember they were constantly fighting, as most siblings will. When his father died, Chavez took his place as *caporal.* He is very protective of us both, especially of Rosa, I will admit, but he is engaged to another girl named Caridad Luz. I love him as I would a son and I owe him a great deal more than loyalty. I owe him my life."

"I understand that he got that scar in a knife fight?"

"*Sí.*" *Don* Enrique sighed heavily and stared off into space. He hesitated so long I wasn't sure if he was going to continue or not, but he finally took another sip of coffee and explained.

"Some time ago we were taking money to our bank when a band of thieves attacked us. Chavez's father was shot down right in front of his son, and I in turn shot the outlaw." As he spoke, *Don* Enrique's right arm brushed instinctively against his revolver. "But two others rushed me from behind and knocked the *pistola* from my hand. They had knives, and one of them would have surely killed me on the spot had not Chavez suddenly thrown his own knife into the man's back. He then fought the other one barehanded."

"And that's when he got cut?"

"*Sí*. But even so he still fared better than the other. Chavez killed that *ladrón* with his own knife. From what they tell me his fiancée, Caridad, has been very understanding and still loves him very much, but sadly Chavez has not been the same man since the wound."

"A little too much on the serious side?" I suggested.

"It is understandable. I suppose one cannot blame him much for that. But he is a good man and an excellent *caporal*."

"I guess you're right," I said. "But he sure doesn't give new folks much of a chance."

"I forgot to mention"—*Señor* Hernandez paused—"the thieves at the bank . . . they were of your people, *americanos*."

That last one gave me something to think on.

The following morning, as usual, I made preparations to scout ahead. I wanted to peruse the next water hole and planned to get an early start. While saddling my horse, I paused to chat with Miguel, who had already started what had now become his morning routine—boots, hat, coffee, a long shave, and then more coffee.

"Which way you headed today?" he asked, splashing water on his face from a bucket perched on the chuck wagon tailboard.

"Want to check up ahead, then swing over to the northwest and have a look-see. Make sure everything's OK."

Miguel lathered his face using an old bone-handled shaving brush.

"I swear, *hombre,* you have got to be the shavingest *vaquero* I ever met," I joked. "And that goes for most cowboys, too," I added.

He adjusted a small mirror that hung from a nail on the side of the chuck wagon. "*¿Tu cres, compadre?*" he asked, feigning surprise.

"Do I mean it?" I replied. "You bet. Hell, most wranglers wouldn't touch a razor on a trail drive, even if they were forced to at gun point. You been looking in that mirror, shavin' and fussin' with that moustache of yours every day since we left the border. Reckon you oughter have it right by now. Besides, ain't no ladies out here to impress, you know."

He adjusted the mirror to keep the glare out of his eyes before replying. "*Cierto,* but how do you say it . . . the cleanliness is next to God."

"Godliness," I said, correcting him.

"*Sí,* godliness," he responded, pointing in the direction of Inocente Vizcara, one of the other *vaqueros* in the outfit, who was just awakening. Admittedly Inocente's unkempt beard did resemble a large bird's nest.

"OK, I don't shave, so you want I should to look like that?" Miguel asked jokingly. "No, not me, I don't want no birdies landing on my face." He laughed, shaking his razor over at Inocente to emphasize his point.

I swung into the saddle and took up the reins. "Well maybe you're right after all, Miguel. How about saving me some of that soap for when I get back."

"You going very far?" Inocente asked as I rode by.

"Three days or so, I reckon."

"Cuidate, hombre," Miguel said, waving good bye, his soap brush still full of lather.

"Thanks. You take care, too." The last thing I remember seeing as I rode off was Inocente arguing with Miguel, and the morning sun reflecting brightly off his shaving mirror.

Chapter Six

Following remote stretches of trail has always been what I enjoy most in life. There's a quiet calm that always comes over a man after hours alone on horseback. The soft rhythmical creaking of the saddle combines with the occasional rattle of canteen or rifle swinging to or fro to create a peaceful melody.

Strangely, even though riding is physically taxing, I've always found it mentally relaxing. Maybe because there're no arguments, no worrisome chatter, no rules to follow, or aggravation.

Even though on the trail it's essential to remain alert to the possibility of danger, eventually it becomes second nature. After a spell on horseback the mind stops fretting and life's focus becomes much clearer. There's just a oneness of man, horse, and Nature.

I'm not sure that it has to do with any special quality the horse might have, though. For one thing, they don't react like pets do. A good dog, for example, practically lives to please its master. You treat it well and you'll have a dependable friend for life. On the other hand, some of the hardest working trail horses I've known would bite, stomp, or kick you silly the first chance they get.

A true horseman never stops adjusting to a

horse's body or reacting to its mood. The trick is to relax, yet maintain control, and the rider who lets his guard down, more often than not, suddenly finds himself afoot. You can't teach a horse dependability, either. A sorry cayuse will spook at every tumbleweed and step in every hole. I suppose that's why it's called horse sense—either a cayuse has it or doesn't.

With a trail-wise horse, life can be downright pleasant. A good pony is sure-footed, agile, and alert. It will walk when it's supposed to, stand if you want it to, and run like blazes when it has to. And that's the way that Morgan bay of mine was. He was as sound as any horse I've ever had.

I'd ridden several hours without any signs of trouble, Indian, outlaw, or otherwise, and figured my current position to be about three days northwest of where the herd was camped. The Morgan could have gone on, but, since he was sweating heavily, I paused alongside the rim of a long gully that sloped off from my right, and down about forty feet.

The area was so hot, dry, and dusty it was a sure bet even the bay was daydreaming about the last creek we'd crossed. I know I was. We'd been searching for signs of water without much luck until finally I noticed the horse flaring his nostrils, as if he were taking a sudden interest in something. Up ahead was a small shallow depression that had formed underneath a smooth rock face overhang. From the way it looked, it promised to be a small collecting basin.

I was concentrating on that overhang when the Morgan suddenly pricked up his ears. The years had given me enough trust in that stallion to know something was wrong. His head turned quickly to the left and almost simultaneously I caught a glint of light reflecting off something metal on a ridge about 100 yards off.

Everything happened so fast I'm still not sure which came first. There was a puff in the dirt near me, and a sharp *crack,* a sound that could have only come from a rifle shot.

I turned in the saddle, drew my Colt, and fired. It was a long ways off to hit anything with a handgun, but mine was purely a reflex action. Turning suddenly like that must have saved me, but the only thing I really remember before everything went black was flinching in pain and grabbing for my head.

I came to, sprawled, face down, at the bottom of the gully, tortured by a loud *buzzing* sound that seemed louder inside my head than it did from its source, a nearby swarm of bees. Even dazed as I was, I knew it wouldn't be smart just to sit up and start moving around. Whoever had shot me might still be around, and I had no way of knowing how long I'd been out.

The dust caked into my mouth and nose as I laid there playing 'possum. It seemed like a good half hour before even I dared open my eyes. After hearing nothing but those bees, I finally felt safe enough to roll over slowly and check myself. Putting a hand to my head, I found the whole right side covered with dried blood. There was no way to tell how much I'd lost, but at least the bones felt intact. Once again I was grateful for the hard head my ma always accused me of having.

Getting up was a chore, but somehow I managed. After taking stock, I realized my pistol was missing from its holster, and began anxiously searching around until I finally found it half buried in the dirt in front of me. The fall must have covered it over with dust.

I probably wouldn't be alive now were it not for my angle of fall. Had my pistol been visible, it would surely have attracted too much attention to ignore. It stood to reason that whoever had bushwhacked me hadn't bothered to enter the gully to make sure I was dead. There was plenty of my blood in the sand, but no boot marks other than my own were present, which confirmed my suspicion.

Head wounds tend to bleed more than other kinds, and many times appear worse than they actually are. That must have been the reason I was mistakenly left for dead. Regardless of how I looked, my head was pounding so bad I had a hard time convincing myself I wasn't still going to end up dead, anyway. I felt downright critical.

Whether barely alive or not, I had lost a lot of blood and had no way of knowing if I was going to pass out again. One thing I did know, though—I had to reach water in a hurry. Unfortunately, in my condition, even the short climb back up that small incline was tough. Just crawling twenty feet winded me so much I had to pause repeatedly, and panted for several minutes at a time before finally reaching the top.

As I feared, my horse was gone and I was left alone, with no help in sight. Worse yet, there was no canteen. I stumbled forward a few yards, and then slid back down toward the overhang, following the sound of the bees. At first I didn't see any sign of water, just that large rock balanced over a six foot round basin-like projection sitting right below the overhang. The bees were buzzing all around it.

After reaching it, I put my back against the wall and pushed hard with my legs against the edge of the rock. It took a couple of tries, but I finally managed to shove it over. Sure enough, a small pool of water had collected underneath.

I removed the bandanna from around my neck, and used it to soak my head. The water was warm and full of sand, but I wasn't in any shape to be particular. I drank my fill, and then curled up under the overhang, falling asleep almost immediately.

I wasn't really sure what time I awoke, or that it was even the same day for that matter. I drank again, this time as much as possible. When it comes to water, I've never believed in small amounts. As far as I'm concerned, it's better to drink all you can, when you can, especially if you may not get another chance. That was especially true in my case since there was nothing around that might be of use to carry water.

I had a powder flask in my shoulder pouch that could have been emptied for that purpose, but it wouldn't hold enough water for a good mouthful. More importantly, if I ran into whoever ambushed me, that gunpowder would be sorely needed.

I took a small rag out of my side pouch and ran it through the pistol barrel, using a small twig as a guide. I also checked the percussion caps, and removed what dust I could. The rest I cleaned with my shirt, after first plugging the cylinder chambers with some beef tallow I always carried in an old snuff box. Pa had taught me to use tallow or beeswax to seal the cylinder off so as to protect the powder from moisture, and to prevent accidental multiple chamber flashes. *Flash*. . . .

I suddenly remembered having seen the rifle flash from up on the hill off to my left, so, after another short rest, it was the first place I headed. After about a seventy-five to a hundred yard climb up the ridge, I came across the body of a dead chestnut mare. Judging by the wounds, my pistol shot had fractured its right front pastern.

At that distance mine had been nothing but a fluke shot. It may have thrown the assassin's aim off, and probably saved my life, but I regretted having hit the mare nevertheless. Whoever shot me finished her off with a head shot, and then stole my bay.

As I sat down next to that dead mare, I resolved to get even, regardless of what it took. I studied the area carefully, taking my time to read the signs. That's when I was reminded of Sprout.

Chapter Seven

The memories came painfully back. Sitting there with the stench of death around me must have triggered the recollections. It, too, had all started with a dead horse. About five years earlier I had been riding south into Texas, alone, and trailing a piebald pack horse. There was word of a big cattle drive out of San Antonio, and I was hoping to sign on before it left.

The area I was riding through had a scarcity of game, and for the last two weeks I'd been forced to live off of old hardtack, and buffalo jerky so tough you could sole a boot with it. I remember it was early afternoon on a landscape that stretched flat out between two horizons.

Those new to the prairie always describe it as wide, but it's more than that. It's so big it hurts the eyes that try to take it all in at once. I've never been to sea, but I imagine the sailor on the deck of his ship must have the same sensation as a rider on the plains, one of personal insignificance when compared to the immense beauty of Nature.

I wasn't searching anything trophy-size that day. I was just looking for something edible, preferably bigger than the palm of my hand, and hopefully meatier. Prairie chicken gets mighty tiresome after a while.

Off in the distance to my right I noticed a small mound that looked out of place. For some reason it seemed the wrong color, or perhaps it was the shape that first attracted my attention. At any rate, there was a chance it might be a kneeling deer or maybe a small stray buffalo down in a wallow. I dismounted and drew my Henry.

I was able to get a good steady bead by laying the rifle across my saddle, but the more I stared across the sights, the stranger that mound looked. My pa had always made a point of teaching me not to shoot until I was sure of the target, even if it meant going without, so I waited. There was no sign of movement, although I felt sure it had to be an animal of some sort. After a minute or two the realization finally set in that what I was aiming at was a downed horse with its saddle still on.

I mounted back up and rode slowly over to it with the rifle slung across my lap. The mound did in fact turn out to be a dead gray gelding, covered in dust and wearing a McClellan saddle. One look at that horse told me there was something very strange about the way it had died.

Although the pony had crippling bullet wounds in its hindquarters and shoulder, they were not lethal ones, and there were no others in its head, chest, or belly. Instead, the horse's throat had been slashed and it had bled out. More unusual still was the trail of blood that led from the neck to another smaller puddle, over a few feet. There were also tracks on the ground spotted with more drops of blood, leading off toward the northwest.

The footprints appeared to have been made by small feet wearing moccasins. The edges of the tracks were still relatively fresh and sharp, unmarked by wildlife, and no water or insects had collected in them. Had the prints been older, the natural process of erosion would have begun to round the edges off, and in all likelihood dust and débris would have filled them in. Whoever it was had passed this way not long before my arrival.

Intrigued, I followed the direction those tracks took for about an hour. From the size and spacing of that lone set of prints, I figured they belonged either to a young boy or perhaps a small woman. Trailing moccasin tracks isn't smart in any man's book, but there was an Army brand and a cavalry saddle on that dead horse, and as usual I was curious.

I knew I should be more careful, but even if the tracks were made by an Indian, I couldn't just let him die out there all alone. Whoever it was obviously was in bad shape, what with the way the feet stumbled around and the amount of blood spilled on the ground.

Like I said, I couldn't be sure who I was following until I finally came upon the body of a young boy, lying facedown on the ground. Although I'd considered the possibility, it still came as a surprise. The lad couldn't have been more than twelve years old! I knelt down and rolled him over to check for a pulse and, to my relief, found him still alive.

"I wonder what the Sam Hill you're doing out here by your lonesome?" I asked myself aloud.

His mouth had blood all around it, but no wound, so I reckoned he'd drunk from the horse's jugular in order to keep himself going. His shirt was torn and there was more blood on his shoulder.

At first I assumed it to have come from the horse, but, as it turned out, there was a bullet hole in his back, hidden up under his long black hair.

I kept some water in a goatskin bag hung on the pack horse and I used it to cool off his head and wash the wounds. I couldn't tell enough from his clothes to know what tribe he was from, but he was a small boy and he was injured, so I cleaned off his face and shaded him from the sun. Indian or not, I felt it wrong to shoot a child, and was not about to abandon him now.

Fortunately the bullet must have been spent before it finally hit him, because the wound wasn't deep. The lead fragment I found just under the skin was easily removed, but, even so, I remembered thinking how painful it must have been for one so young.

I sat there holding the boy until he regained consciousness, and then poured some water in his mouth. After a drop or two moistened his lips, he started to drink on his own, and opened his eyes. They were sky blue!

"Well now, what do we have here?" I asked.

He gasped and tried weakly to push himself away. My smile reassured him a little, and after a short time he finally calmed down.

"Whoa, there, sprout, relax, you'll be all right. Just take it easy and drink slowly."

He went limp, took a couple more swallows, and then collapsed back to sleep without saying a word. I carried him over to the horses and made him a bed out of my blankets and saddle.

He slept for the rest of the afternoon and all through the night, awaking only once to take some broth made from the ocotillo powder and other herbs I always carried. He was too dehydrated even to pass water till late the next morning. While he rested, I secured the horses, made some coffee, and kept watch all night with my Henry by my side. He was only a boy, but he was also a frightened plains Indian, a fact I wasn't about to take for granted.

"Sure wish you spoke some English so I can decide what to do with you," I said the next morning. He had been awake for over an hour and was trying to eat a little of the breakfast I'd fixed, but mostly he just drank. What food he did manage to keep down had to be chewed over and over, and swallowed slowly.

He had a shrunken stomach from not having eaten for so long. I'd been that way once before, and, contrary to what most folks might think, when a person's that starved, as much as he may want to, it's hard to get a whole lot to stay down. That kind of deprivation makes even the simple act of eating a painful task.

The boy had hollowed eyes and stared back at me with a blank and distant expression.

"I don't even know your name, where you're from, where you're going to, or anything," I said, more to myself than him. "And what in the world I'm going to do with you is beyond me. Sure don't fancy riding right into a Comanche camp with you. Hell, I'm not even sure you're all Injun. Never saw one with blue eyes before."

"Kiowa," he said, looking up from his plate for a moment.

"How's that?" I asked. "You understood that? Can you speak English?"

He nodded his head. "Kiowa say my white

parents killed years ago in buffalo stampede. I found in small hole near their wagon with Father on top of me. He died trying to save me from being crushed. The Kiowas heard my cries, and Wolf Tail, second cousin to Santank, took me as his own."

"Santank, the chief? I heard of him."

"Yes. He is Kaitsenko."

"What's that? Sorry, I don't follow."

"The Kaisenko are the Real Dogs, the Society of Ten Bravest. They lead the tribe in battle, and are sworn to fight to victory or death. Three of the Real Dogs wear red cloth bands, six wear red skin of elk, and the leader, Chief Sitting Bear, wears a black skin from neck to ground."

"I get it. So you grew up with this cousin, Wolf Tail."

"Well, I was raised by Pipe Smoking Girl, a Kiowa medicine woman, but Wolf Tail has always called me his son," he said proudly.

"OK, so what name do you go by now, boy?" I asked, filling my cup back up with coffee.

He responded in Kiowa, which I didn't speak, later explaining in English that it meant something like Buffalo Calf Wailing.

"Well, I can't go around callin' you Sobbing Buffalo or Buffalo Crying Calf or whatever," I said. "Don't you remember your real family's name?"

"Now Kiowa my family. Only one," he said stubbornly.

"Look, sprout, if you're going to ride with me, I'll have to call you something easy enough for both of us."

"What sprout mean?" he asked.

"That? Well, it's sort of a nickname. You know,

like a bean sprout, new growth . . . youth?" I tried to explain.

"Fine," he said, nodding his head.

"Fine what?"

"From now on I am Sprout."

I shrugged my shoulders. At least it was simple enough, and for the time being neither he nor I were in any mood to argue.

"You know, for someone who doesn't remember his own name you sure speak English well enough."

"Some I remember, some Wolf Tail teach me. Rest I learn from . . . uh . . . half-breed men who lived among us. At one time white men were welcomed in Kiowa camps. First ones act more like us humans. But after that, others come to take buffalo and rob us of our lands. They are like mosquitoes, coming in swarms to suck Kiowa life blood dry. Chief Santank soon learn truth. He always keep me near whenever he deal with white men. Santank wanted to see how men who translate for Long Knives lie. White men never knew I understand English when I play nearby them. Santank and Wolf Tail are wise men, not fools. They get better meaning from white words with me around to help," he said proudly.

"Don't you want to go back to your real people now?" I asked innocently. "Maybe your family had kinfolk that are still around. The Army might have a list of people who are missing and any relatives that are still looking."

"Kiowa are my family!" he answered angrily. "And Long Knives cannot be trusted. They have no respect for the people, or the land. They do not know what is right."

"Aren't you being a little hard. After all, they can't all be bad."

"Who do you think shot me? Why do you think I am alone out here?" he said, adjusting the sling I had made for his shoulder.

"What do you mean by that?" I asked.

"Ever since soldiers come, they have tried to kill us or put us on reservations. Kiowa always walk the earth free, north from the land of the Dakota and south to Méjico. No limits, no reservations. My people were traveling south, away from Fort Sill when Long Knives attack us. We had harmed no one. Wolf Tail wanted to go south to hunt over land that was once ours. Just to hunt. But soldiers attack us without warning. When we see them coming, we tried to run, not fight."

"It's a little hard to imagine Kiowa braves running," I commented.

"Our braves were not afraid for themselves, never. Kiowa fear no men in battle, but they do worry about women and children. When Long Knives started shooting, our men tried to lead them away. A group of soldiers caught me. One was about to shoot me when his captain stopped him. He saw my face and blue color to eyes, as you did, he say to me that I am now *rescued* and gave orders to take me away."

"What about the others in the group you were with? Where are they?" I asked, fearing I might already know the answer.

"The captain made me watch as soldiers killed all the Kiowas they had captured."

"Not the women and children?"

"Yes," he answered quietly, the pain evident in

his expression. "Pipe Smoking Girl, too," he added sadly.

"So how did you end up here?" I asked.

"First chance I get, I steal knife from soldier next to me. I stick him in arm and broke free. They shot me." He touched his shoulder. "But I ride away. Try to find my people."

I shook my head in disbelief. I knew how painful that wound was but amazingly he never showed it. At least not to me.

We camped another full day until he was strong enough to ride.

"I'm headed south, Sprout," I said, "so I guess you'll have to come with me. At least until I can find a place to drop you off."

He stood his ground and shook his head. "North."

"Sorry. Not headed that way. Can't afford to lose any more time," I replied. "Besides, I'm not sure I would be smart to ride around Indian Territory looking for Kiowas. It's not worth the risk." It was a harsh comment to make to him, but I was really just thinking out loud. "Come on, Sprout, you've got no choice." I turned the horses around and slowly walked south, figuring he'd follow sooner or later.

I was wrong. When I looked back, he was already several hundred yards away on foot, headed in the opposite direction.

"Of all the stubborn. . . ." I stared at him a while, and then, cursing to myself, reluctantly turned the horses north.

Later, as I shifted the packs between the two mounts, I looked over at the boy cautiously.

"He's a bit spirited," I said, referring to the piebald. "Sure you can handle him?"

By way of reply, he simply grabbed hold of the pack horse's mane, swung up on the paint, and galloped around in circles. It was an incredible display of horsemanship for one so young, highlighted by him sliding off the horse's far side and hanging on by the stirrup and cinch strap. He was riding at a dead run, facing backward while lying completely horizontal. He had practically vanished from sight when viewed from my side. It was more than enough to convince me of his riding ability.

We traveled together for almost a week, until crossing a river about 200 miles from Fort Sill. We had trailed the rest of the Kiowas, who'd escaped, to a clump of trees at the bend of a small creekbed.

Sprout was perched in front of me, just behind the saddle horn, my arms around him. The sight ahead had us both paralyzed. There, lined up along the bank, in a straight row of fifteen, were the remaining Kiowa braves. They were side-by-side, and all were dead. Worse yet, they had each been decapitated! Every brave was stretched out, legs apart, with his head stuck between them, staring forward in a grisly display of the white man's cruelty.

For the first time in my adult life I felt shame.

While I didn't ask, it was evident from the boy's expression that Wolf Tail was among the dead. Sprout took it all in without shedding a tear.

"I now ride with you," was all he said for the next three days.

After that there was no being shed of the boy. Sprout stuck to me tighter than a hungry tick on a brown dog. He wouldn't have gone back to an Army fort now if I'd threatened him at gun point, so I ended up taking him south with me. At first my excuse was that nobody in these parts was likely to adopt a young Kiowa, regardless of his eye color, but after a while I truly began to favor his company.

The boy was a surprisingly fast learner.

I soon found myself having fun sharing what I knew with him. Since I'd never had a younger brother, I discovered, to my surprise, that it was not all take and no give. In fact, during the year and a half we rode together, Sprout taught me many things back, such as reading sign and trick riding, Injun style.

We continued on south and finally joined that cattle drive just north of San Antonio. Old Amos Simpson was in charge. Not surprisingly he was reluctant at first to take on a Kiowa, young boy or not. Fortunately his partner, Dave Randall, had served for a year with my uncle Zeke while in the military, under Doniphan, and recognized our family name.

In December of 1846, Colonel Alexander Doniphan and his Missouri Mounted Volunteers had ridden south from New Mexico to reinforce Wool's division in northern Mexico. For nearly six months the Missouri Mounted trekked some 2,000 miles straight across Mexico to the Gulf Coast, winning battle after battle.

To hear Uncle Zeke tell it, they were a real rowdy bunch. "No uniforms, no pay, and no discipline, but no finer group of fighting men ever lived," he'd bragged. "Doniphan was just a lawyer and amateur tactician, but he shore was one natural-born leader. At Brazito we was surprised by Mexican forces, but Doniphan managed to beat them back in less than an hour. And later, in a battle outside Chihuahua, when we was outnumbered three to one, the colonel single-handedly turned what could have been a real disaster into total victory."

Dave Randall later told me that he counted 300 dead Mexicans when the smoke finally cleared. The Missouri Mounted Volunteers had lost only three men.

"Amos, if this lad's kin to Zeke, you can bank on his word," Randall told his partner. "If he says there won't be a problem with the boy and is personally willing to vouch for him, then, Injun or not, we'd best take him in. You know as well as I do that Zeke once saved my life, and, since I was the one who pulled you out of the Canadian that time back in 'Sixty-One, well, I guess that means you sort of owe him, too."

Under the circumstances, it was hard to argue with Dave's logic, so Amos finally gave in and hired us both. The men were apprehensive at first but any doubts about Sprout soon vanished and the novelty of having a friendly Kiowa scout eventually caught on. Over the next several weeks, the men began chipping in one by one with bits and pieces of clothing, although no one could ever break the boy of his habit of wearing moccasins.

Sprout learned to drive cattle, to rope and to brand, but, more often than not, Simpson used the boy to help out with what he knew best and enjoyed most, namely hunting and scouting. With Sprout along there always seemed to be an extra rabbit, squirrel, or deer for the pot. We ate better on that drive than most, due in large part to the boy's efforts.

A lot can happen when you trail with someone for over a year, and we eventually wound up as close as real kin. Sprout started nagging me for almost four months solid to help him get a sidearm and holster of his own. I finally broke down and promised to buy one at the next town we passed.

"I don't know why folks are always referring to the patience of the noble savage," I'd joke. "Hell, you've been pestering me more than a thirsty mosquito in summer. Look, Buffalo Grove is just ahead. I'm going after some supplies while Lucky gets our horses re-shod. After that maybe, just maybe, I'll see about finding a six-gun for you." The boy's face lit up like a campfire.

Early the next morning Lucky Crawford, Sprout, and I rode to town, but as always the boy stopped cold about two miles out, refusing to go any farther. He had learned to trust the others in the outfit and was all right as long as we were alone on the trail, but even after all this time he avoided strangers and refused to go anywhere near a fort or town. Reluctantly we left him camped near a small creek, figuring we'd be gone no more than a couple of hours.

Once in town I ran my errands for the boss, and then headed over to the saloon, while Lucky saw to our horses.

We met later on at the pharmacy and bought some rolling paper and tobacco, and a bottle of oil of clove for Dave Randall's sore tooth. It was there in the store that Lucky pointed out a Starr

Arms double-cocking .44 they had on display in their glass cabinet. It wasn't the newest or most accurate piece I'd ever seen, but it was dependable enough. More importantly, the shop owner let me have it at a good price.

"The kid's sure gonna light up when he sees that," Lucky commented to me, smiling.

"Yeah, well he deserves it. He works hard."

"Sure does. Say, you fixin' to adopt him permanent like?"

"Never thought about it much. He's a little old, ain't he?" I asked.

"Nah. And come to think of it, you ain't gettin' any younger." He laughed.

"Very funny. But, maybe you're right." I paused to think it over. "You know, now that you've brought it up, might be kinda nice to give the kid my name. I'll think I'll chew on it some."

We rode back to the clump of trees near the creek where we'd left Sprout, but, as soon as we arrived, it was obvious something was very wrong. His horse was nowhere in sight for one thing, and there were buzzards circling overhead.

"I've got a bad feeling about this, Lucky," I said.

"I'm way ahead o' you, partner." His gun was already drawn and cocked.

We split up and rode into the trees from opposite directions. That's when we spotted him, face down on the ground, dead. I dismounted and quickly hurried to his side. When I rolled him over, I found three horribly large triangular knife wounds, running right through his chest. It was as if he'd been speared clear through.

Lucky holstered his gun and dismounted.

"Whoever it was is long gone. Must have been

after his horse. See they's two sets of tracks riding in, but three heading away to the south. The boy could have been napping . . . or maybe just thought it was us returning," he added.

"They must have been riding double and saw a chance to steal his horse. He didn't even have a chance, Lucky. Three men against one kid!"

"Who'd do something like that?" he asked sadly.

"I don't know, but, one thing's for sure, if I ever catch up with them, they'll wish they'd decided to walk out of here, instead."

"Hope to God I'm with you when that day comes." Lucky turned back and pulled a small folding shovel out from his pack.

We buried Sprout among the trees, under a large overhanging branch. It was a clean peaceful spot, and the shade was nice and cool.

Lucky and I followed their tracks for several days until it began to rain and we were forced to turn back. We never did find those three. Even now, although all that was behind me, I still hoped our trails would someday cross so I could even things up for Sprout.

Chapter Eight

The small drop of blood that snaked its way into my left eye caused my eyelid to twitch, snapping me right back to the present. My head hurt and my neck ached, but the pain also served another purpose. It made me mad. Someone had bushwhacked me, stolen my horse, and caused another to die needlessly. I vowed to find the miserable coyote responsible and make him suffer.

I tried to stand up but my head was spinning so much I almost fell over backward. My stomach cramped, and it took a full minute or two before my eyes could focus again. For the moment, at least, it was clear that I'd have to worry more about survival than vengeance, so I knelt down, removed my knife from its scabbard, and began to butcher the dead horse.

Horse meat isn't something I'd normally prefer for supper, but I knew it was going to be a long walk back to camp across difficult terrain, with no assurance of finding any game. Besides, in the shape I was in, even if I did find something worthy enough to take aim at with my handgun, I might not be steady enough to hit it.

I started a fire and cooked the meat. What I didn't eat would be dried for the trail. I needed to regain my strength but my stomach felt as if it were full of paint remover, and I had to fight to keep down the grub. I almost threw up the first couple of mouthfuls, but fortunately things settled down after a few more bites. I shook my head a little, wondering why Apaches and Frenchmen favor horse meat so much. But I had eaten worse and, in my condition, was grateful just to have meat available, regardless of what kind it was. I still wouldn't consider it my favorite, though, not by a long sight.

Something inside of me was urging me to return to the Hernandez camp as soon as possible, but I decided it was better to take things slow, to be careful. The *mejicanos* have an old saying to the effect that being first to arrive isn't near as important as knowing how to get there. It made more sense to go slow and return alive in one piece, than it did to die rushing into things, so I decided to get a good night's sleep and leave the following morning.

At dawn the next day I started out on what promised to be a long, hard, uphill trek. By the end of the second day on foot, I knew something had happened to the rest of the *vaqueros*. Chavez and his men should have started the herd moving in my direction, yet there was still no sign of them. I had been gone about three days before getting shot, and although it was probably too early yet for anyone to be overly concerned about me, I knew the *caporal*. Chavez was a cautious man, but he was also one who would react swiftly at the first sign of danger. By now he should have at least sent someone to scout me out, and my trail shouldn't have been too hard to follow.

While it was possible that *Don* Enrique and

Chavez had decided to double back to their original course, it was unlikely, being as how the *don* was not one to change his mind once a considered decision had been made. If, on the other hand Chavez had managed to convince him otherwise, they would have sent someone to let me know about it. That being the case the rider would have reached my position by now.

When I curled up that night, I decided to cut due east in the morning and then head south, rather than simply backtracking. It would mean several days of hard climbing over much more difficult ground, but it would save me considerable time. Besides, I now wanted to approach the camp from high ground, with a clear view of what I was heading into.

A couple more days of hard but uneventful travel finally brought me to the base of a vertical rock face on the far side of the cañon where the *vaqueros* had been camped. To save time I'd cut cross country, but now, assuming the outfit was still camped in the same place, I would have to scale that one final wall.

As a boy I loved to climb anything in sight, be it tree, hill, or the barn out back. Right now, though, I was tired and nowhere near enthusiastic about the uphill climb, so I sat down for a good fifteen minutes to rest, study the wall, and plan the ascent. It didn't look especially steep or dangerous, but I wasn't about to risk breaking my neck in a fall.

I made sure my gun was tied down tight, and then reversed the spurs on my boots to project downward past the heels, hoping they'd give me better traction during the ascent. My hands had become well calloused over the years, but as an added precaution I removed an old pair of work gloves from the bottom of my shoulder pouch. Then, using my boot knife, I carefully cut away the fingers and trimmed the leather from the glove arm down to the wrist. When I'd finished, I had two gloves that hopefully would protect my hands from the sharp rock, while at the same time leaving my fingers free to grasp with.

I chewed a few strips of dried horse meat for energy and took several deep breaths before beginning the ascent. As worn down as I felt, I was grateful the climb went well. It turned out the slope wasn't very steep after all and there were plenty of wide crevices for hands and feet. Within two hours I had easily reached a position just below the summit. With my goal finally in sight I felt a renewed surge of energy and rushed quickly toward the top. A little too quickly perhaps.

Suddenly, as I swung my body over to grab for another handhold, the wall around me suddenly collapsed. Once committed there was no way back. Rock and gravel peeled away and in one terrible, gut-retching instant I found myself dangling in mid-air, facing out away from the wall. I was suspended totally by my right arm, my hand wedged into a small crack in the rock face.

I tried to dig in, flailing back with my heels, but the hard rock had given way to a sandy, loose gravel that wouldn't allow me to gain a decent purchase. Desperately I threw my weight across my shoulder and succeeded in rolling over to a toe-in position, face flat against the wall. For the moment, at least, I needed to rest.

My grip was firm enough, but I knew it wouldn't last forever, so I searched around anxiously for another hand- or foothold. The wall had magically transformed itself into such a soft smooth surface that nothing within reach would support my weight. There was one small projection nearby that offered some hope, but it was off to my left and several feet above my head, just fatally out of reach.

I tried to control my breathing, calm down, and think. My knife wouldn't help since the whole area was now much too sandy. I thought about using my holster, but even if I could manage to unbuckle and rebuckle it with one hand, the belt would be too wide and awkward to be of any use. Trying to pull my body up with my right arm still wouldn't allow me to reach that one small outcrop, and I couldn't swing my legs up to it. I looked up at that rock helplessly. There it was, solidly embedded in the wall, projecting out only a few feet from the top, but just enough out of reach to spell my downfall. And that would be precisely the correct word I thought grimly—*downfall*.

Sand shifted into my face, forcing me to reach over with my left hand to wipe my eyes, face, and neck free of débris. When my fingers drifted across the shoulder strap holding my travel pouch, my heart skipped and I breathed a small sigh of relief. There might still be a chance.

I put the strap in my mouth so as not to risk dropping it as I eased it off over my head. My hat was hanging over my back by its tie string, but fortunately they didn't tangle. Grabbing the bag in my left hand, I let go of my bite and examined the pouch strap. It was braided rawhide and an integral part of the pouch, easily able to support my weight, for a short time at least.

I began to swing the strap while holding firmly

onto the bag. It took several attempts before I was able to shift my position enough to throw overhead, but then just as suddenly as hope is given, it can be taken away. The rock face began shifting again under my right hand and I watched in terror as the slit began to open. Desperately I began to swing, throwing that strap furiously, over and over again, hoping for a miracle. My scream echoed from the cañon walls as my right hand broke away from the rock.

It took several seconds before I even opened my eyes. It felt like my heart had jumped into my throat and my ears pounded, but I was alive, suspended by the pouch strap wrapped around my left hand. Luckily it had caught the projection on the last throw. Not about to wait for anything else to go wrong, I flung myself over, quickly grabbed hold with my right hand, and pulled myself up to solid rock. The bag itself made a good foothold, allowing me to push on over the top.

I reached down for the pouch and pulled it up after me. Rolling over, I clutched it to my body and went limp. The last thing I did before passing into a deep sleep was give that old beat-up leather pack a long, hard kiss.

I must have laid there a full hour or so before I was finally able to continue on. I got up and brushed myself off, grateful the climb was over. It was downhill all the way now, with a clear view of the valley below.

Unfortunately, before I got even halfway down into the valley, I knew the camp had been deserted. Buzzards circled the corpses of several dead horses and what little was left of Joaquin and Chango's wagons had been burned into two ashen piles.

Tracks left by the herd led out of the valley and away to the southwest. I found still others made by a smaller group heading back southeast, opposite our original direction. The double sets of furrows behind this second group spoke volumes. After the camp had been attacked and the herd rustled, the *vaqueros* must have turned back toward San Rafael, carrying their wounded on horse-drawn travois.

I came upon three fresh gravesites, not far from the burned out wagons. Inscriptions had been crudely carved into a piece of wood nailed to a tree branch. The first one read simply: JOAQUIN GUTTIEREZ—NUESTRO COCINERO Y AMIGO.

I shook my head sadly and moved on to the other two. The sentiment on these markers was quite different. ASESINO Y LADRÓN was all that had been recorded, but then murderer and thief said it all anyway.

I rummaged around the remains of both wagons and found two sacks of beans that were only slightly singed, and half a sack of cornmeal. There were also three or four canteens lying around that could still hold water. There weren't any horses left alive and the only rifle I could find was too badly damaged to be of any use.

I scavenged what little I could from the camp while all the time looking for clues as to how the attack had occurred and who might be responsible. The herd had trampled most of the area and any remaining sign had been spoiled by the fire.

It did seem, though, that the *vaqueros* had been

caught totally by surprise, and I found that very unusual. This valley wasn't known to many others, and I couldn't understand how a band of outlaws that big could have approached the herd without *Don* Enrique's men noticing.

Chavez always made a point of making sure the night rider stayed awake in order to prevent something like this from happening. I wondered what had happened to that rider.

It wasn't long before I noticed a clump of scrub brush that didn't match its surroundings. Although most of the dead horses and goats were scattered at the other end of camp, the buzzards seemed to be paying an unusual amount of attention to that same patch of scrub. As I neared it, the smell was so bad I knew right off that I'd found the missing sentry.

I pulled my bandanna up over my face, and then kicked the bushes back. The flies were so thick I had to back off and grab a hunk of brush to shoo them away. I found what I'd expected but it was of little comfort. One of the *mejicanos* lay curled on the ground with another dead body alongside. The *vaquero* had part of his head crushed in, probably by a rifle stock, and it took me a moment or so before I realized it was Gregorio.

I couldn't recognize the other. He was obviously an American, but no one I'd ever met. From what I could tell, Gregorio had been jumped while riding the herd, and had been knocked from his horse. They must have tried to knife Gregorio, instead of shooting him, so as not to alert the rest. Taking on a *vaquero* with a knife is never a good idea, however, even by surprise at night, and Gregorio had very good reflexes.

The cowboy laying there had a six-inch blade sticking out of his chest and an empty sheath on his belt, so it figured that, when they had struggled, Gregorio must have disarmed his attacker and then turned his own knife back on him. Although this one got what he deserved, another of the bastards must have clubbed Gregorio from behind.

I rolled the dead outlaw over and searched him for identification, for some clue as to whom he was or whom he rode with. Unfortunately there was nothing in his pockets except an old tobacco pouch, a bent hoof pick, and a poker chip from a place called the Golden Goose Saloon, in Gila City. Not much to go on.

Without giving it much thought, I pocketed the poker chip and rolled the outlaw out of the way. Others might be more charitable about such things, but I wasn't about to waste my efforts burying him. Gregorio, however, was my friend and deserved better, as does any good man who goes down fighting. I wanted to bury him alongside of Joaquin, but, given the condition the body was in, it would have been hard to carry him by hand, so I went back to camp in search of a blanket.

I returned to cover the *vaquero* and then, using a plank torn off of Chango's wagon, dragged his remains back to the campsite and began to dig a grave. I managed to rummage up a shovel out from under the wreckage. It was burned but still intact, and served its purpose.

The ground wasn't especially hard, but the work was. I knew it wasn't my fault, but guilt has a funny way of creeping into one's bones. I was the scout for the outfit. It had been my job to pick a safe route, avoid trouble, and get the herd through intact. I had argued for the change of direction, chosen the campsite, and now my recommendations had led to all this. Good men were dead, others injured, and the lives of two good families were faced with ruin, all because they had trusted me.

Logic told me that I wasn't responsible for the crimes of a band of renegades, but I still couldn't shake the feeling that I was somehow to blame. The more I dug, the harder the ground seemed. I was tired of burying friends and family.

Chapter Nine

Standing over Gregorio's grave with shovel in hand started me wondering if someone would be as kind to me when my time came, and, judging by what I'd been through, there was a distinct possibility that could be sooner rather than later. Just as that thought crossed my mind, a rustling sound erupted from the bushes nearby, and a branch snapped. My right hand dropped to my side, but before my Colt broke leather, Bruto, one of Chango Lopez's two mules, walked through the thicket and out into the open.

I was so relieved when he approached, I actually laughed aloud.

"You purt' near scared the daylights out of me, old fellow," I said, rubbing his forehead. "How in blazes did you manage to get away?"

His harness and bridle were still in place, with the reins trailing on the ground behind. I replaced them up over his back, so he wouldn't step on them, and quickly checked him over. There were a few minor cuts and scratches but fortunately nothing major. Bruto was snorting anxiously, so I stroked his mane, trying to calm the both of us down.

Even though cowboys work mostly range-crossed grade horses, every rider I'd ever met had a strong opinion about what they considered the best breed of horse. Cowboys will spend hours around a campfire arguing the merits of the wild mustang over the thoroughbred, or comparing Arabs to Appaloosas. While *vaqueros* are basically no different, Chango Lopez was especially particular about his choice. He rode mules.

In actual fact, Chango rode what had to be the biggest brace of jack mules in the Southwest. I'd seen large mules before when I hauled supplies to outposts in the Kansas Territory for Russell, Majors, and Waddell, but nothing like the pair Chango used. On a bet Rogelio once measured their front hoofs. They turned out to be twice as big across as those of the biggest gelding in the remuda.

Chango liked to alternate between the two mules, Bruto and Bobo, using one to pull his supply wagon while he rode the other. I'm not sure which job the mules preferred, but there couldn't have been much of a difference, not given his size.

I once asked Miguel how Chango had come across a matched pair that big.

"Oh, he had them when we met him," Miguel replied. "*Don* Enrique was returning from a sale in Tampico with a bunch of us when we come across Chango, alone, with that wagon and those two mules. His *padre* was a great *herrero* . . . you know, a blacksmith . . . but he was shot to death. A *bandido* everyone called El Tuerto once rode through their pueblo looking for someone to shoe his horse. When Chango's father finish the job and ask for his money, El Tuerto shoot him, instead of paying. So Chango, he go look for this *assesino,* and later he find him in Los Senos del

Diablo, a very bad place near Saltillo. Even the *Federales* don't go there."

"What happened?" I asked.

"Chango, he find this man in a *cantina* with two others, drinking tequila and playing the cards. El Tuerto had a gun, sure, but Chango had his father's hammer. The other *bandidos* joined in the fight, too, but Chango . . . he used that hammer on them. They say you could slide what was left of those three under the door. Both mules and the wagon belong to the two men who were playing poker with El Tuerto. I guess Chango not feel like walking home, so he just took them. Chango didn't any longer want to stay at home after his *padre*'s death, so he rode away to look for other job. After they met, *Don* Enrique give him a job and he has been with us ever since. But you know, nobody ever give him the hard time or make fun of his choosing to ride mules."

Of that I had no doubt.

Bruto, the mule, stood quietly in front of me as I bent over to pick up the shovel I'd dropped when he surprised me. I laughed again, wondering who'd been more startled, him or me. Even though my nerves were still on edge, that's not always a bad way to feel when you're alone in the wild. It heightens the senses and keeps one alert for danger. At least this time it did, for, as I stood there in front of that mule, the sudden flicker of his ear and the toss of his head warned me something was wrong.

Any other time I probably wouldn't have even noticed it, but that sixth sense of mine had suddenly begun to act up again. I listened carefully, but heard nothing unusual. Even so it seemed that the mule was standing a trifle too still and he kept staring straight at me without blinking. Something was definitely wrong, but it was something I couldn't put my finger on. I strained to hear, see, or even smell something, anything that might be out of the ordinary. It was while I was looking at that old jack that I finally caught the reflection in his eye. My blood almost froze at the realization that I was watching three Apaches closing in silently from behind, captured crystal clear in that mule's big old round pupil.

They rushed me just as I turned, swinging that shovel. It caught the first one with a crushing blow to the side of his head that killed him instantly. There was still time to draw my pistol, and the Navy Colt bucked in my hand, sending a slug squarely into the chest of the second brave. Although a lethal shot, it didn't stop his forward motion, and the Indian plowed right into me, knocking the gun from my hand and sending me spinning off to the side.

Fortunately his dead body landed on top of my gun, putting it out of reach of the last Apache. The fall also blocked the Indian from reaching me before I had a chance to recover, forcing him to cross over the body. Judging by the six-inch knife in his hand, it was only pure luck that had saved me from being gutted on the spot.

That luck was short-lived, however, since Apache warriors don't waste time. This one turned back around to rush me, but I quickly reached down and pulled my Bowie from its boot sheath, forcing him back a step. It made him pause to reconsider as only fools rush someone with a blade. My stomach muscles tightened as I remembered Uncle Zeke's advice on knife fighting.

"Expect to get cut, and don't ever play fair. Try to git outta there, but, iffen you cain't, use whatever you can to win, 'cause in a knife fight the winner sometimes ends up in worse shape than the loser."

This battle was now going to be one on one. Had there been any other Apaches around I'd surely have been dead by now. These three had probably fled the reservation and then later spotted the campfire. More likely than not they were only after the mule and some guns, but this Apache clearly wasn't about to quit now. There was nowhere for me to go but right into it.

We circled, twisting and turning, thrusting and parrying, trying to feel each other out. Some men use a knife like a sword, slashing or jabbing, trying for the quick kill, but the more experienced ones make small circular slicing movements, keeping the blade in close. They prefer to cut up an opponent little by little, bleeding them out enough to make them helpless, before finally going in for the kill.

This Apache was strong and very determined, as most are. He had obviously used his blade many times before, but then so had I, and there was no way I was going to do anything foolish like kicking at him, which would risk a severed leg muscle. Nor would I just stand there facing him straight on.

All I offered my opponent was a constantly moving and well-guarded side view. Even so, his blade nicked my left arm twice, and a couple of times came uncomfortably close to my throat. We locked grips once, but I managed to drop down onto my back while at the same time throwing my feet up into his chest. By holding onto his arms, I managed to flip him backward over my head. Although I came up fairly quickly, he had already jumped back to his feet in what wrestlers call a "kip up". It was a beautiful move, but one I was in no mood to appreciate.

We traded blows for a while with both hands and feet. I managed to backhand him with my left hand while at the same time sweeping his legs out from under him with my foot. But once again he was quick to recover, and rolled out of my reach. I was tiring quickly, and the Apache began taking advantage of that fact by grappling more, all the time trying to wrestle the Bowie knife from my grasp.

Once again Uncle Zeke's words came back. "Use whatever you can. Whatever it takes." So I let the Apache lock up with me once again, and then fell to the ground in a side roll, taking him down with me. We rolled over several times and my face was pushed down into the ground before we finally pulled each other straight back up to our feet.

Neither of us let loose of the other the whole time, until we finally came to a stop and stared, face to face, at each other, arms outstretched and locked. When the Apache made eye contact with me, I shrugged as if to apologize. The Indian was staring me squarely in the eye with a puzzled look when I sprayed his face with all the dirt I'd swallowed when we'd rolled over.

Instinctively his hands jerked up to his face as he tried quickly to wipe his eyes. When he finally looked back at me, it was with an expression of bewilderment. He looked slowly down to my Bowie knife, now embedded in his belly, and then back up at me. With his hand clutching the hilt, he fell over backward, dead.

Chapter Ten

For obvious reasons I didn't hang around the camp any longer. I briefly considered going after the rustlers alone, but it was out of the question. I had almost no supplies, little ammunition, and the mule wasn't fast enough to catch the herd. San Rafael was the only logical place to go since there I could remount, reëquip, and find help. Riding Bruto would be slower than a horse, but at least he was solid and dependable, and would get me back to town. Once I managed to climb up on that enormous back of his, that is.

We must have been quite a sight; a *gringo* riding bareback on a big jack mule, weighed down with canteens and assorted bean sacks all tied to a wagon harness. Although the trip back to San Rafael wasn't all that hard, when we finally arrived in town a little past noon, I was again on foot. I had been leading the mule for the last half hour, on account of his having thrown a front shoe hard enough to crack the hoof. I couldn't help wondering what else would go wrong. After all I'd been through, a blacksmith's own mule goes and cracks a hoof on me! It made me remember that old saying about the cobbler's kid's shoes.

After watering Bruto at one of the troughs scattered along the street, I left him hitched to a post outside of the livery with instructions to take good care of him.

I wanted to clean up, change clothes, and get something to eat, so I headed for the mercantile store, just down the street about four buildings away, on the side opposite the town's only boarding house. The street was fairly deserted, but that wasn't unusual for this time of day.

Folks around these parts like to *siesta,* so things usually quiet down from noon until early evening. Those that weren't asleep were probably inside the *cantina* drinking or outside of town at the local social club, partaking of whatever pleasures of the flesh were available, heat allowing.

I was dog tired and hungry to boot, so, after entering the shop, the first thing I did was pull a large can of sliced pears down off the top shelf. Prying it open with a clasp knife the owner kept tied to a nail for such purposes, I gulped all the juice, and then used the point of the knife blade to pull out the pears. That sugary juice hit the spot and felt better than anything I could remember for quite sometime.

I finished the pears and took a box of ammunition off the counter and pocketed it away in my shoulder pouch. The storekeeper went by the name of Sam Martin. We'd been on good terms before, but, since he was usually a talkative sort, I found it strange that I'd been in the store almost ten minutes without him saying a word. He just kept staring at me from behind the counter like I was a ghost or something. I was about to ask him for a little extra credit toward a new pair of pants and a shirt, when Rosa Hernandez walked in.

After all I'd been through, she was more than just a sight for tired eyes, so I walked over and smiled. I was going to ask about her father when she suddenly smacked me right across the face with her riding crop.

"How dare you! How could you, after we all trusted you?" she cried. Rosa was about to hit me again even though I was still stunned from her first quirting.

"Hey, what was that for?" I said, grabbing her forearm in defense.

"You dare ask me that after what you did to my father and his men? You knew how important that herd was to us! Let go of me." She was struggling to get her arm free, while at the same time kicking my left shin, hard.

"*Ouch!* Look, I don't know what you're talking about. Someone bushwhacked me out there and left me for dead. Here, just look at my head if you don't believe me." I let go and pointed. "And I mean up here on top, not where you just whipped me."

"Rodrigo was there when you rode in and ambushed our men. The man who led the thieves was masked, but Rodrigo recognized you nevertheless. The big *gringo* with the bay horse is what he said." She was still angry, although maybe now not quite as much.

"I swear to you, Rosa, it wasn't me. Think about it, would it make any sense for me to come back here if it had been?" I asked. "The man who shot me and stole my horse was obviously part of the gang that rustled your herd. He left me for dead out there. It was all I could do to get back here in one piece. Trust me, I would never do anything that would bring you or your father any harm." I was speaking more softly now.

She looked at me and raised her eyebrows slightly as if reconsidering the situation.

I raised my hands up to her shoulders and looked into her eyes. "I'm telling you the truth."

"Even if I were to believe you, Chavez would not," she said after a moment of hesitation. "He is mad because after you convinced my father to change directions, you rode safely away. He says you had planned all along to leave them there in a trap."

"Well, now you know he's wrong," I said firmly. "Maybe I can talk to him or your father. What do you think?"

"They wouldn't give you the chance," Rosa replied, shaking her head.

I glanced around uncomfortably. If the *vaqueros* were as worked up as Rosa described, they'd likely shoot first and ask questions later. The last thing I wanted was to be forced into fighting men I'd ridden with, especially those I'd grown to respect.

I went to the window and checked the street. It was almost deserted, except for a passing buckboard and a woman on her way to the seamstress. Thankfully none of the *vaqueros* was anywhere in sight.

"I can't just stay here waiting for them to come over and lynch me."

"If you can get to your horse and ride out of here, maybe I could meet you somewhere? After I explain things to my father," she offered.

I shook my head. "I don't want you in the middle of this. Besides, I don't have a horse, mine was stolen, remember? I had to ride in on one of Chango's mules." I looked quickly around the store, and then grabbed a pair of saddlebags down off the shelf. After cramming as much as I could into them, I turned to Rosa. "I'll have to let you pay for this now, but I swear I'll be back to settle things. You have my word on that."

She looked into my eyes. "I believe you. Don't be foolish. Just go away now, quick, and don't come back."

Years of hard work and loneliness suddenly came to a head. Under different circumstances there might have been a chance for a good life here with someone who mattered. I don't know why, but I somehow felt there still could be. Rosa made my heart ache every time I saw her, but it was a good kind of ache, the longing kind. She was a woman who any man would be proud of, yet any chance I might have had with her was about to be destroyed by a rotten dry-gulcher and a band of murdering horse thieves.

On impulse, I grabbed her in my arms and, before she had a chance to object, I kissed her, hard and long. There are some things that just happen, things you can't control. At first she was surprised, but she soon relaxed into my embrace and kissed me back. My heart raced.

"I'm leaving. I've no choice about that," I said, stroking her hair. "But I'm coming back. That you can count on. I'm innocent, and now I've got a special reason to prove it, one more important than the law or my reputation. I've got you. Believe me, I'll be back with the herd, or the money for it, or I'll die trying."

"I believe you will," she said quickly. "Try to

reach my horse, *querido,* it's over at the stable. You can ride away. If nobody else sees, maybe I can convince Chavez, later, that he was wrong about you."

I nodded back at her and rechecked the window.

"Cuidate, carino," she whispered as I darted out the door.

The street was still empty as I headed toward the stable, but before I made it halfway across one of the *vaqueros,* Ricardo, suddenly emerged from the café across the street. He took one look at me and immediately went for his gun.

"Ricardo, no!" I yelled frantically. *"Esperate* . . . wait!" But it was no use, his gun was already drawn. He fired as I ducked left, and luckily he missed. I drew and fired, aiming low, hoping just to knock him off balance.

He was young and enthusiastic. After riding with him only a short time I'd grown fond of his good nature. I knew he was only reacting as any top hand would. He believed me to be the outlaw who had shot his boss, and he was protecting the brand. There was no way I was going to kill him if I could help it, but unfortunately for Ricardo I couldn't let him keep on shooting at me, either.

My bullet caught his left thigh, spun him around, and knocked him down. I knew our gunfire would awake the dead, and in a minute or so every *vaquero* in town would be out in the street. My eyes caught sight of another horse tied to the hitching post at the end of the street, a big chocolate roan, saddled and waiting. I headed over to it, hitting the saddle on the run.

Just as expected, several *vaqueros* poured out of the *cantina,* pointing at Ricardo and shouting to one another. Their shots rang out behind me as I lit a shuck out of town at full tilt. I didn't have time to look back, and had to gallop away with my feet hanging out of the short stirrups on that roan's *mejicano* saddle. It was a full hour before I was finally able to stop to adjust them to my own length and to plan my next move.

The *mejicano* saddle on that roan was a large elaborate affair and in order to lengthen its stirrups to accommodate my feet, I had to untie long rawhide strings interwoven along the leathers. Rather than using snaps or buckles like those on my other saddles, these stirrup leathers laced up crosswise like a lumberjack boot. It took me several minutes just to figure them out.

I still had the saddlebags with me I'd taken from the store, but this saddle had its own leather *mochillas* built in behind the cantle of its seat. Instead of tying leather bags down behind the seat with straps like a Texas or Colorado saddle, the pouches on the *mejicano silla de montar* actually formed the entire rear part of the saddle.

After the way things had worked out so far, I knew I'd be riding this rig for a while, so I studied it carefully. The saddle seat was an uncovered wooden tree with a couple of wide straps crisscrossing over it and then disappearing down into the fenders and skirts. Unlike my saddle this one had a split up the middle similar to the McClellan seat the cavalry uses.

I'd once seen a similar saddle used by some trappers down from Canada, but I always thought it looked mighty uncomfortable. "Ball buster" is the expression some of the Army boys use to describe that type of saddle, but everyone admits it's easier on the horse. That split up the middle almost had me thinking about going bareback, but the *vaqueros* seemed to favor it. Surprisingly I'd just rode a full hour without any appreciable side effects, so I decided to stop worrying, figuring it couldn't be any worse than that old rawhide saddle I'd first left home on.

One thing I did fancy, however, was the pommel, or saddle horn. This one was a large, pure white, dish-like affair as broad around as my two hands would be with fingers fully open. The Texas roping saddles I was used to have a hard but much smaller pommel horn, suited for the type of work they're used for. The big Mexican pommel on this saddle was made for longer reatas and a different style of cattle roping. It angled up higher and was much wider.

There was a Spencer rifle in the scabbard on the right side of the saddle and, I noticed with some amusement, a large machete in the sheath that hung from the left side pinned under the stirrup leather.

The gelding snorted and flipped his head up to shoo away a small bee buzzing around his ear. I had no complaints whatsoever about my luck in finding that cayuse all saddled and waiting. I'd admired his stamina and agility ever since I first saw Chavez working with him. As far as horses go, he was eventempered and remarkably fast.

One thing I did miss, however, was the feel of leather reins in my hand. Chavez had this roan fitted out with one of those colorfully braided but uncomfortably stiff rope affairs that come up short into a knot, right where I usually held my hands. By my way of thinking, the bit was also too harsh on the mouth, and I vowed to replace it the first chance I got with a Texas-style leather bridle and curb bit.

I started making plans. I'd promised Rosa to go after the herd, and that was one promise I aimed to keep. The problem was I had no idea where the horses would be by now. All I had to go on was the poker chip I'd found from The Golden Goose Saloon in Gila City, a pretty slim clue. It might just have been an old good luck piece, or its presence merely a coincidence. Maybe one of the rustlers had gambled there once and simply forgot to return the chip.

On the other hand it could mean the rustlers had passed through Gila City, and that they might return by the same route. Or if not, maybe someone around town could supply me with some bit of information that would be of help. I had no choice, I didn't know where else to go, so I headed for Gila City.

Besides the fact that the poker chip was the only clue I had, there was the additional problem of what to do once I found the gang. One man can't do much against that many outlaws, especially when they include the sort of cold-blooded killers who would slit a man's throat from behind.

One thing more was certain. Chavez wasn't the type to quit something once he got started. He believed me responsible for stealing his herd and almost killing *Don* Enrique. Now that I'd shot Ricardo, there wasn't a single *vaquero* who'd believe me. They were sure to be fast on my trail, and I knew, if they caught me before I reached the herd, I'd swing from the nearest tree.

While I knew the *vaqueros* could be loyal friends, I was equally convinced that they'd be fearsome opponents. The more I thought about it, the more sense it made to use that fact to my advantage. I wouldn't let them catch me, but nothing said I couldn't let them follow.

In fact, a bunch of armed and angry *mejicanos* might just come in handy when I found the rustlers. That is, if I found the rustlers. The trick would be to keep well ahead of the *vaqueros,* all the while making myself so hard to follow that it would buy me enough time to investigate. Still, I had to do so without letting them lose my trail for good.

I was more grateful than ever for all the tricks Sprout had taught me, and hoped that Chavez and his men were good trackers. Good, that is, but not too good.

So, I started a game of cat and mouse. At times my trail would seem to disappear, while at others conveniently reappear just as suddenly. My tracks led into blind cañons, backtracked along rivers, and sometimes seemed to head off in several different directions at once. Ultimately, however, my trail led west. West toward Gila City.

Chapter Eleven

Funny how the mind works when you're tired. I'd been riding for several days straight without stopping, with little water and even less food. I was being hunted by what could turn out to be a Mexican lynch mob. It was a toss up as to who was dustier, the horse or me, and to top it off, when I finally reached Gila City, there was a manure smell in the air so strong the odor reached me even before the town came into view. Normally the stench would have been damned disagreeable if not downright intolerable, but for some strange reason it just made me smile. It was a funny reaction, but I guess it reminded me of the time ten of us from the old L Bar got into an argument over different kinds of critter smells.

We'd been driving cattle toward Kansas for over a month and had stopped for the night. After the usual evening pleasantries we were bedding down when Frank Kendall bent over to move his saddle. Frank's rump was practically sticking right in Pinto Ward's face when he broke wind. Damned if Pinto didn't fall over backward trying to get out of the way. He was so mad Pinto would have shot Frank right on the spot were it not for the rest of us laughing ourselves half to death.

That, of course, started the boys off on a night-long debate on the virtues of different animal leavings. As expected, most of the cowboys were convinced that cow patties smelled the sweetest, whereas those of us who worked as wranglers sang the virtues of the noble steed's road apples. The buffalo chip was discussed, but for argument's sake, and since there wasn't an Indian among us at the time, the buffalo was left in the same group as cattle.

There were a couple of boys from Tennessee who actually claimed they preferred the smell of pig droppings to all others, and it took half the night for them to convince us they were really serious.

We finally stopped arguing when Chester Martin shouted: "Sheep! Sheep stinks the worst, and ain't no one convincin' me otherwise!"

The fact we had spent the better part of three hours trying to decide which manure smelled the best, not the worst, seemed to have eluded him. But then again, it seemed an honorable way for us all to agree on something, even those who had never even seen a sheep. Besides, nobody on that drive wanted to be the one to disagree with Chester Martin. It was hard enough getting along with Ches when he was in a good mood, without risking getting him into a bad one, so we all unanimously agreed—sheep stinks the worst!

I remember that bunch as always arguing about something stupid, but we did have good times together. Now, with all there was to worry about, I found myself daydreaming about something that silly. Funny how the mind works sometimes.

As I rode into the southeast edge of town, the

livery was the first building that appeared. It was about as dirty as everything else there. Piled all around the stable were several twelve-foot-high stacks full of old urine-soaked hay and horse droppings, not to mention several thousand stable flies.

There was a circular corral out in front made of split logs nailed to a dozen or so vertical poles, but there wasn't a single straight post in the whole ring. Out in back was a long rectangular lean-to shack with about thirty standing stalls and a half dozen box stalls.

I rode up to a trough made from an old barrel that had been cut lengthwise and turned on its side, and watered the horse. An old bearded groom was brushing out a chestnut gelding hitched to one of the corral posts. I noticed the man wore an old black stovepipe hat that had a rather sizable chunk torn out of it.

I dismounted, loosened the cinch, and pulled the saddle.

The old man caught me glancing at his hat, spit, and grinned back at me. "A swaybacked hammerheaded old jack took a bite out of it about a year back."

I nodded, wondering why he hadn't bothered to buy another hat. But then again, he didn't bother to swat away the flies that were constantly landing on him, either.

"You the owner here?"

"Am now. Previous one got shot after selling a blind grulla to the wrong feller. Ah told him he ought to give the money back." He shook his head. "Guess he learned the hard way . . . the customer's always right. 'Specially when he's holdin' a double-barreled sawed-off. The name's Lijah. Just toss your tack on that pole over there. You need anything special?"

"Well, I'd like him brushed down, and when you feed him, mix some corn in with the hay."

"Cost you extra."

"Figured as much," I said, tossing him a coin. "I may be leaving soon, so how about making sure he's saddled back up again after he's cooled off and fed."

Elijah spat a stream of tobacco juice from his chaw and wiped his mouth with the back of his hand. "Looks like he's been rode hard." He dried his hand on the front of his shirt. Judging by his shirt it must have been a regular habit.

"Maybe so, but it don't mean I want him put up wet." My reply was meant to insure things got done right. "By the way, is there a saloon around here called The Golden Goose?" I asked.

"Sure is, if you feel like blowing all your loot." He used his hat to point with. "Go on down about four buildings and turn left. You cain't miss it." I must have looked worse than I thought because he added: "Some folks clean up and shave at the Chinaman's place. Up the street over there, second building." Obviously he wasn't one of them.

Right then a wash would have felt swell, but with Chavez and his men hot on my trail I couldn't spare the time. At least for now I'd have to stay just as I was.

Elijah began untying the chestnut. When I started to leave, he turned the horse back toward the stable. The EH brand on the gelding's rump caught my eye as he swung around.

"Say, how about that," I said. "I have a friend

that rides a gelding just like that one. Swear they could be twins. Even has the same three socks."

"That so," Elijah said. "Small world, ain't it?"

"Well it probably isn't my friend's. Short fat friendly chap with wide sideburns?"

"Nah, 'way off." He shrugged. "This one's a tall thin sort with a full beard. Carries a big bone-handled knife in a chest rig. You know . . . the kind they call an Arkansas toothpick. Rode in with two others. Kind of a hardcase iffen you ask me." Apparently rethinking what he'd just said to me, a total stranger, he quickly added: "But then again ain't none o' my business." He quickly disappeared with the gelding back into the barn.

It wasn't far to the saloon, but the street was so miserably dusty I reconsidered stopping for that bath. I ended up deciding against it, though. For me to earn the confidence of rustlers and bushwhackers I'd have to give the impression of someone on the run. *Well, at least that much was true,* I thought to myself grimly.

I paused at the front of the saloon and peered through the double doors before entering. The Golden Goose was anything but golden, the same being true of the rest of Gila City.

At one point the town had boomed, the mines attracting fortune-seekers from all over. But that was years ago. The glory days had long passed, and those that hadn't already left town were probably now too far down on their luck to get out. Either that or they stayed on in order to prey on the misfortunes of others, like vultures cleaning a carcass.

Whoever owned this saloon was obviously more interested in stripping the remainder of his customers of their money than in building new business. That was made clear enough from listening to the number of complaints and curses coming from the gaming tables I passed on the way to the bar.

The place was in total disarray, and the stench of stale beer was thick enough to cut with a Bowie. In its day the saloon may have been high tone, but no longer. The carpeting was faded and torn, the mirror over the bar cracked, and most of the stairs leading up to the second floor were warped. The piano player at the far corner was doing a fair job of "Steamboat to Natchez", especially considering his piano had two keys missing.

At the other end of the bar, alongside the wall, was a large barrel of water with a gourd ladle, and next to it a side of beef on a spit. A loaf of hard-baked bread and a knife lay on a small table right under a sign that read: Sandwiches. Eat at your own risk! I drank some water from the barrel, rather than ordering a hard drink from the bar. For what I had in mind I would need what little money I kept stashed in the neck bag I always carried under my shirt.

I was so hungry I cared more about quantity than quality, and cut myself a large, hopefully clean hunk of beef from the spit, and slapped it on the bread. They were right about the risk, both the bread and the beef turned out to be about as tough as the room I was surveying.

There were about twenty round gaming tables in the place. At the center table four men were playing poker, and, from what I could see from behind, the cowboy in the middle fit the description Elijah had given me of the one riding the EH-branded gelding.

My plan was simple enough. After joining their game, I would try to make them believe I was broke and out of luck. Maybe I could get in the position of playing them for a job. If they were convinced that I was on the run and let me join up, there was a chance they might lead me to the herd. Or, if the horses had already been sold, then maybe I could use them to track the money.

There was nothing to lose. My name had to be cleared or I'd never have a chance with Rosa, and I still had the *vaqueros* to deal with. I knew Chavez wasn't the kind to quit, and I had no desire to repeat a showdown with men like Miguel, Armando, and Francisco.

As soon as one of the players busted out of the game, I walked over to their table.

"Closed game or can anyone sit in?" I asked.

The tall thin man in the middle wore a broad flat sombrero and wide leather wrist straps. The bone-handled knife slung across his chest was at least fourteen inches long and double-bladed. The two flat sides of the blade had been built up, with high supporting ridges that seemed sharp enough to cut with. The whole affair tapered wickedly to a thick point.

When that cowpoke looked up at me, my blood froze. Hanging around his neck was a Kiowa talisman on a rawhide thong, a hand-sewn beaded affair representing an eagle. Such a necklace was supposed to ward off evil, and protect one from harm. Each design was unique and especially designed by a certain medicine woman. I knew all this because the talisman that cowboy was wearing had once belonged to Sprout.

Staying calm after seeing that eagle was the hardest thing I've ever had to do. I wanted to fly right across that table and rip his liver out with my bare hands, but, since I had to find out where the herd was, for now it would have to wait.

I avoided staring at him by quickly switching my gaze over to the second cowboy seated immediately to his left. This one was wearing stovepipe chaps, a horsehair vest, and carried a large pocket watch on a gold chain. Pulling out a chair, I tossed my pouch on the table and addressed myself to him.

"Not much there, but maybe it'll build some."

"Welcome to try, but don't get your hopes up," he replied.

"The name's Pete, Pete Evans. That's Ed Jenkins," he said, indicating the third man, "and this here's Comanche Reynolds." His talkativeness was surprising, but helpful. Out here most men usually kept things to themselves, offering up only what was absolutely necessary.

Turning back to the one called Reynolds, I asked quietly: "You called that for some special reason?"

He looked up at me through narrowed eyes and fingered the necklace. It was unusual to have questions posed by strangers, but after a short pause he answered anyway.

"Took this off a Comanche brave during a wagon train attack in 'Fifty-Nine. Got him just as he was about to let fly an arrow at me. Been called that ever since."

That's when I knew for sure he was a damned liar.

I nodded as if duly impressed and began to check my cards. Poker was one skill I was proficient at, and before long it was obvious to me that these three weren't anywhere near as good as they thought they were.

Chapter Twelve

It didn't take long to catch on to the system they were using to cheat whoever joined the game. The three were much too sure of themselves, and made the mistake of judging me solely by appearance. Most cowboys pride themselves on their card savvy, and these men were no exception. Truth is, even though cowboys brag a lot about cards, when it comes to poker, miners have got them beat hands down. And I for one was no stranger to pick and shovel.

The stakes tend to be higher around miners. When a claim is good, the chips fly, and, when the mine's played out, they bet for future shares of the next lode. Sure, cowboys gamble along the trail, often for wages received at the end of the drive, but that's usually not very much. Riders are always busy doing something with the herd and that distracts from the game, so cards are really just a diversion on the trail. Some bosses won't even allow their men a friendly game during a drive.

Miners on the other hand are frequently stranded at their claims for weeks on end, and up north it can be all winter. Red dog, five-card, and seven-card draw can become a part of their lives, a way to keep from going crazy.

For about seven straight months five of us had worked a gold claim near Bannack City, Idaho. We lived in three patched tents and a makeshift cabin thrown together with leftover boards. From sunup to sundown we dug and sifted to exhaustion, and, when we dragged ourselves back at night, it was usually to a simple dinner of sourdough and old salt pork, or beans and dried apples.

There wasn't anything else to do, and nowhere to go to blow off steam, so we constantly played cards. Jebediah Edwards, Sam Prescott, Philly Nash, and I played as much as we could, and as well as anyone else around, but it was Riverboat Chantal who usually won the pot. We played almost every night for a solid month and nightly I lost about half of everything I had dug up to him.

Chantal supposedly grew up on the river. Or so they said. Jebediah once told me that Riverboat had dealt up and down the Mississippi for years, and I had good reason to believe him. That is until one evening when, after finishing almost a fifth of sour mash, Riverboat confessed the truth to me about his past.

"Mah father was a sailor and mah mother a French-Creole. They died during the pox outbreak when Ah was real young, and that left me in N' Orl'ans. Ah growed up workin' odd jobs in a social club in the red district what belonged to a friend o' mah father. You know the type," he said, looking somewhat distracted.

I nodded at him.

"Those gurls shore was purty."

"I can imagine," I said. "Go on."

"Well there was this small casino next door that Ah hung around regular. That's where Ah got to know Pierre One-Ear, the greatest card-sharp ever was."

"And he taught you?" I asked.

"Eventually, but not right off. He knew Ah used to trade things around town, so Pierre decided to swap me his card tricks, one at a time, in exchange for pokes with some of the girls Ah worked with. Yessir, old One-Ear really liked the ladies, but after he got his ear bit off in a fight, the decent ones shied away from him. So ya see he sorely needed mah help. Ah remember, there was this one gal who worked the club by the name of Candice. She liked fancy perfumes so Ah always traded her that for Pierre. It worked like this. From time to time Ah lifted jewelry from some of the house patrons to trade for perfume which Ah gave to her. She then lent her favor to Pierre and he'd teach me another trick, an' so on. 'Ventually Ah got Pierre to teach me a good bit, but he went and got shot before Ah could get real knowledgeable. The rest Ah sort of picked up as Ah went along."

He paused to watch Philly Nash pick out his fingernails across the room. It was a constant habit that always drove Riverboat crazy, especially since Philly had fingernails that were twice as long as any man we'd ever seen.

"No wonder they call him Filly," Chantal growled. "Sure as hell wouldn't call him Stallion . . . not with them girly nails of his. Beats me how he gets any work done wearin' 'em long like that," he added.

"Don't think he spells it with an F, Riverboat," I observed. "I think he's called Philly 'cause his family hails from Philadelphia."

"Well, whatever. But, if you ask me, for a miner

he spends more time diggin' 'round in those nails o' his than he does in the ground."

I could only nod in agreement. Admittedly it was kind of hard to explain.

Chantal took another swig and continued on. "Truth is Ah hate boats. Hell, Ah get sick just lookin' at a glass of water. You couldn't get me on a paddle boat, raft, or canoe now iffen you was to threaten me with a buffalo gun. The only time Ah ever rode one, Ah throwed up so much Ah begged the captain to put me out of mah mis'ry. It was so disgustin' the crew finally tossed me overboard. To top it off, Ah cain't swim and almost drowned. Iffen it warn't fur a log floatin' by what drug me ashore, you'd be the only one here doin' the winnin' from those two."

"Then why in the world do they call you Riverboat?" I asked, puzzled.

Chantal had finished his jug so I passed him the rest of the one I was drinking from. He gulped down another slug and continued on.

"Simple. One time, over in Tucson, Ah was playing with this whiskey vendor who knew Ah hailed from N' Orl'ans. Kind of an unlucky feller when it came to cards, but he wouldn't never admit it to himself. Just naturally assumed Ah had to be a Mississippi boat gambler. It was he what tagged me with the name Riverboat. Soon everybody started calling me that, and afterwards it just seemed easier to go along with folks."

That was simple enough to understand. A lot of men out West had changed their names for one reason or another. "Guess it's easier to handle losin' all your money if you think you were taken in by a sharp," I added.

"Well you ought to know, kid." He smiled as he pulled in the pot we'd been playing for. "Look, Ah'm gonna educate you proper like. After all, there's not much else to do around here at night and you sorely need the help."

"Yeah, you must get pretty bored winning all my money like that," I replied.

Over the next few months I learned that there are more ways to cheat at cards than there are cattle in Texas. Chantal taught me about marking cards and reflective rings, bent cards, stacking a deck, palming, and about shills. Getting the other fellow to cut the cards to your advantage and bottom dealing were just basics for him. When I finally decided to leave the good life and ride out, I had won back almost all that I had originally lost. In spite of that Riverboat seemed truly sad to see me go.

"Heard say the mark of a good teacher is to be outdone by the pupil. You sure make me proud now, boy, but why don't you stick around and try to win back the rest?" he asked.

"Nope. You taught me enough to know there's bound to be a few tricks you've held out on me," I said. He just smiled back. "Besides, Sam and Philly need to hang onto a little something for their old age," I joked. "With both of us staying on, you know it wouldn't be fair. As it is now practically all Jeb has left is an old photo of that half-naked actress, Ada Menken."

Riverboat helped me tie down my bedroll.

"Saw her once in person, ya know," he said. "Fine-lookin' lady, but she warn't really naked. Just wears a skin-colored outfit. But it don't matter much. First chance these boys git, they'll prob'ly spend whatever's left on easy women and hard licur."

"Likely I'll do the same," I said. "You take care now."

He patted my horse and bid me a safe journey. It was the last I ever saw of him.

A few years later I learned from Shiloh Marks, an old friend of Jebediah's, that a cave-in had taken Sam, Philly, and Riverboat. Jeb had escaped with a crushed hip, but luckily could still get around on a cane. In fact, he was one of the men who later proved the local sheriff, a man named Henry Amos Plummer, was actually the ringleader of a gang of claim-jumpers.

The cave-in had been no accident, and Jebediah knew it. There had been several robberies in the area and for quite a while he'd suspected the sheriff. As long as Jeb lived, he represented a threat to the gang, so Plummer finally sent two of his deputies to kill Jeb. When they failed in their subsequent attempt, they were caught and brought to trial. Faced with the prospect of life imprisonment, they confessed to being in Plummer's outlaw gang.

Even with a bad hip, Jebediah later led the posse that captured the crooked sheriff. His friend, Shiloh Marks, told me they decided to hang Plummer on the very same gallows he'd originally helped to build. That he died like a coward was no surprise.

Marks also told me that Jeb eventually moved back to Illinois where he married some widow who owned a feed and grain supply. Shiloh said she had Jeb so buffaloed he'd given him the picture of Ada to hold onto, lest his wife catch him with it.

What those men taught me during their card games back in Idaho had served me well over the years. The trick with these three cowboys here, in Gila City, would not be to win all their money at once, but rather to keep playing. To stay in the game. I needed time to convince them I was on the wrong side of the law and desperately in need of a job. They had to be made to believe I could somehow be of use to them. I wanted my game play to seem inept in order to keep drawing the game on, but without busting out.

Their strategy might have fooled most men, but Evans was overly confident. The three were so intent on cheating others, they didn't expect it to be done to them and it was no chore at all to keep ahead of Reynolds and his pals. I'd simply fold early on the set-ups to avoid big losses, win a few small hands, building my holdings a little at a time.

Whenever they tried to give me too good a hand, I'd make a bonehead play, like drawing unsuccessfully to a straight instead of sticking with two pair. If I got too far ahead, I intentionally lost and made a big fuss about it. I kept some money to play with, enough to keep them interested, but not enough to be suspicious.

"Look, fellers, I really need a job and ain't particular," I finally remarked. "So if you three need a fourth, I'm as good as the next feller and ain't choosy about usin' my gun, if need be."

"Say, why don't you just throw that fancy Colt of yours into the pot and liven things up some?" Evans asked, avoiding the subject.

"Nope, I reckon I'll stick with it," I replied. "Too hard to come by in the first place, if you know what I mean." I winked, hoping the way it was said would give them the wrong idea.

"Yeah, only one way a drifter gets a fine piece like that, and it ain't workin' cows," Jenkins commented, taking the bait. He was the better-looking of the three, clean-shaven and square-jawed. His shoulder-length brown hair draped down from under a large fedora, and his tanned complexion highlighted blue eyes that must have won over more than a few women. His good looks sure as hell wouldn't influence my opinion of him, though.

"Won it in a contest," I said, giving an exaggerated smile to the saloon girl serving beers to the table.

"Sure you did. And I'll bet the feller you *won* it off of really misses it."

For some reason Pete Evans felt real comfortable joking with me like that. Strange, considering we'd only just met.

"Don't suppose so, seein' as how he's dead now," I answered, bending the truth a bit.

"Figured as much," Jenkins mumbled. "So, ever done any stage work?"

"Some. But I got tired of worrying about getting lead poisoning," I answered. It wasn't all a lie since, at one point in my past, I'd ridden shotgun for Henry Wells for almost eight straight months.

"Yeah, I know what you mean," said Pete, joining in. "Gettin' a lot rougher these days. We got a sweet deal going now, though."

"Evans, you talk too much. Just shut up and play." Comanche Reynolds clearly was the one in charge.

Pete Evans had left the door open a little so to speak, so I jumped in, fearing there might not be another chance. "Look, if something's up . . . if you've got something good going . . . maybe you could use an extra hand. Sure could use the work and, like I said, just what kind don't bother me much."

"Maybe Davies could . . . ," Pete started to say, but Reynolds cut him off.

"We work alone," he said sternly.

There it was. There wasn't going to be another chance, and, if I tried to push the issue, it would appear too suspicious. I had to come up with another plan and quick.

"Well, can't blame a feller for tryin'," I said. "So how about we up the pot a little. Maybe my luck will change. After all, if you can't join 'em, beat 'em so to speak." I wasn't joking.

Considering how bad I'd been playing, the three were readily agreeable, anxious to finish me off so they could move on to richer prey. They never knew what hit them. Within two hours they had lost all their money, plus Jenkins's gold watch. Not in one pot, mind you, but quick enough so they couldn't figure out how I'd managed it. I had made sure they were completely cleaned out. I wanted them broke, and so mad they'd be sure to come after me.

The last hand of seven-card I dealt was sweet. Evans and Jenkins both had two pair up and a matching down card. Reynolds had two queens showing, and a queen and a pair of kings buried. All I was showing was a five, an eight, and two threes. They bet the pot. But I'd buried two other fives and dealt myself the last five as my final down card. Four of a kind beat them all.

"Well, you never can figure it," I gloated. "Guess this was my lucky day after all. So, since there's nothing keeping me here now, I guess I'll be seeing you boys."

Without waiting for a reply, I scooped up the money and left, hurrying over to the stable. I was careful to watch my back on the way out of the saloon. I didn't want to give them the slightest opportunity to get at me while we were still in town.

The roan was saddled and waiting for me. I was in a rush, and, since I needed more lead time, I drank long and hard right from the horse trough, and then quickly filled my canteen. Before leaving there were two other things I needed.

"Elijah, I'm gonna want that shovel and a set of hobbles if you can spare 'em," I said. The gold eagle I tossed his way more than helped convince him. "By the way, if anyone asks about me, it ought to cost them both time and money to find out I'm headed west. That way." I pointed to make sure he knew what I meant. "But especially time, if you get my drift. An hour or two ought to do it."

He nodded back at me, indicating that he understood me all too well.

"Oh, and no need to mention about the shovel to them," I added.

"None of mah business," he answered, shaking his head. "But good luck at whatever ya got in mind, anyway," he added. "Ah reckon you'll need it."

I knew my choices were limited. Trying to follow

those three would have been out of the question. I had no way of knowing for sure if they'd ever even return to the herd, and, if they did, they'd surely be watching their back trail. Since I hadn't gained their confidence and had failed to convince them to let me ride with them, I really had only one option left: somehow to force them to reveal the herd's location to me. I knew that wouldn't be easy, and I'd have to hightail it for a while, because what I had in mind for them couldn't be done in town.

After leaving the livery stable, it took several hours of hard riding to find a stretch of ground suitable for my purpose. Reynolds and his pals were so angry when I left, it was an easy bet they'd follow, which was precisely what I now wanted.

Three men armed against one doesn't make for good odds in anyone's book, so I wanted an edge. Some years ago a small band of Mescaleros had wiped out a cavalry patrol five times their number. The Apaches saw them coming, buried some of their own men alive, and then waited. When the troopers passed by, the Indians sprang up out of the ground and attacked the patrol from both sides.

Describing the attack, Uncle Zeke once told me: "Remember, most folks don't pay attention to detail, they just see what they want or expect to. Soldiers often have too high a notion of themselves, but the Apache knows that plannin' and surprise in battle will make up fer a whole heap of men."

I don't know why that particular story of his stuck in my mind, but I reckoned, if the trick had worked once, it could work again, so I began looking around for the right patch of dirt.

After finding a good spot, I stopped and hobbled the roan. Since I didn't know how he'd react to gunfire, I also ground-tied him to a hefty rock. I chose a place with a big tree nearby that I hoped would act as yet another distraction, giving Reynold's group something else to look at.

It took almost twenty minutes to dig a big enough trench. I angled it between the base of the tree and the horse, opposite the side I expected them to ride up from. It took another ten minutes to clean the area of tracks and other sign, but before I got down in that hole, I did two more things. First I buried the shovel. Then, foolish as it might seem, I took off my holster and hung it on the saddle horn, right out in plain view.

I had my reasons. The gun belt would attract their attention up, away from the ground, and over to the saddle, making them think I was unarmed. I hoped it would give them a false sense of security. Also, I had no intention of getting that Navy Colt of mine all choked with dust. Instead, I unsheathed the rifle from the saddle scabbard, and wrapped it in my shirt. After that I laid down in the hole, with the rifle along side, and pulled some sagebrush and tumbleweed over for cover. I figured they wouldn't be looking down, not when searching for someone my size. All I had to do now was wait.

White men deal with time differently from Indians. Seems like we're always expecting things to happen quickly. Heck, it's gotten so bad a lot of folks can't live without constantly having to check their watches. The Indian on the other hand doesn't worry about time like we do. They just wait, preferring to let things take their own natural course.

Having to lie half naked in a hole in hot ground would drive an impatient man crazy, but I had learned enough from Sprout not to make that mistake. Once I was down in there, I tried to relax and not worry about what might happen or when. Reynolds could be right on my tail, or he might still be in town. Though I felt fairly sure that he would follow me, all I could do now was wait and listen. Wait in that hot dirty hole with my rifle and the bugs. In the meantime, the trick would be to remain still, not cramp up, and to be ready to move when need be.

I lost track of time, but it was beginning to cool off when I finally heard them ride up.

"There's his horse. I don't see him around, but be careful." It was Pete Evans doing the talking, as usual.

"Wonder where he is?" said Jenkins.

The one I wanted most was Reynolds, who finally spoke out.

"I don't like this. Where the devil could he have gotten to? Even if he had another horse waiting, he sure as hell wouldn't leave that fancy hogleg o' his behind like that."

I flexed my muscles in grim anticipation and tried extra hard not to make any sound.

"Well, I'm gonna grab that gun afore he gets back, that's for damn' sure." It was Evans again. "Here, Ed, hold these reins fur me," he said.

Because of the way I had that roan tied to the tree, in order to reach the holster without getting hung up in the branches he would have to dismount and walk around the horse. And that's exactly what he did.

"What makes you think you'll get to keep that thumb-buster?" Jenkins asked.

" 'Cause I got to it first," he replied.

Just as Evans started reaching for the holster, I came out of the ground, screaming as loud as I could. The horses all spooked, trying to buck their riders and Evans froze in his tracks. I was on him in a second, cold cocking him with the butt of my rifle. I was lucky, and he went down limper than a wet rag.

Just as planned I'd come up right between the tree, my horse, and the others. The roan was both hobbled and ground-tied, and couldn't move even if it had wanted to. On the other hand, it was a while before Reynolds and Jenkins could gain control of their horses, more than enough time for me to get behind the roan and, using it for cover, replace the holster on my hip. I stood there with my rifle cocked across the saddle and waited.

They finally settled their broncos down and turned to face the rifle I had pointed at them.

"Jenkins, you may still have a chance to get out of this with your hide intact, so, if I were you, I'd just sit there and try real hard not to flinch. If you even blink, I'll blow you right off that kak and not think twice. It's Reynolds I want."

"What do you mean? Who the hell are you and what do you want with me?" Comanche asked, somewhat puzzled. He was trying to position himself as best as he could but his horse was still jumpy.

"Look, we were just riding this way when we saw your horse. Thought something was wrong and you might be hurt. Is this what we get for trying to help out?"

"Nice try," I said. "That might've worked on someone else, but the truth is I don't give a damn what the hell you were doing. You'll likely die today, Reynolds, but it won't be for trying to bushwhack me over a lousy card game."

"What is it, then? What are you talking about? We never even met before today, so what's your problem?"

I had to hand it to him, he seemed more unsure than scared.

"Happened a long time ago. About the same time you started going by the name of Comanche," I said, walking around the horse. I switched the rifle to my left side, cocked it, and held it pointed at Ed Jenkins, who so far was just sitting still and listening.

"I don't get it. If you aim to kill me, you can at least let me in on why."

"I will . . . in due time," I said. "By the way, that Indian necklace you wear around your neck, the one you're so proud of." He glanced down to his chest. "It ain't Comanche, it's Kiowa."

"What the hell makes you such an Injun expert?" he said angrily. He fingered the talisman with his left hand without letting the reins drop.

"Because the boy it belonged to was my friend."

He was still looking down at his chest as I spoke, but, when the meaning of my words sunk in, he slowly looked back up at me. From the way he stared back at me, I knew I had the right man. I could see fear in his eyes for the first time, just as I'm sure he read death in mine. Reynolds hesitated a second or two, and then went for the pistol at his side.

He started the draw but I finished it. At that range I couldn't miss, and the last thing Reynolds ever saw before the bullet took his head off was the hatred in my eyes.

Jenkins decided to make his play, too. He must have figured I was too distracted, or that my left hand would be slower with a rifle, but he was wrong. As soon as he cleared leather, I let loose the Spencer right into his chest. He toppled off the horse and fell to the ground, flat on his back. He didn't die right off, though, and, as I stood over him, I could see he was trying to tell me something. I leaned closer.

"It were Reynold's idea," he gasped. "But Pierce and I was with him. Felt bad about the boy even if he were an Injun, but we was drunk. When the kid hit Reynolds, the other two kinda went loco. Couldn't stop 'em." He coughed.

"Pierce who?" I asked.

"Pierce held him while Reynolds knifed him clean through." Jenkins was dripping blood from his nose and his breathing was much heavier.

"What about the other one . . . Evans?" I asked.

"Pete? Talks too much. Weren't even there, just us three. We met Evans a year later." He was breathing so bad I was barely able to understand what he was saying.

"Where can I find this Pierce now? And what about later on? Tell me about the EH brand on Reynold's horse, and about the herd you rustled," I asked, but it was no use. I was talking to a dead man.

Chapter Thirteen

When Pete Evans finally came to, he found himself flat on his back with both arms and legs bound firmly to the stakes I'd driven into the ground while he was unconscious. I'd found some pigging strings in the saddlebags, the rawhide straps that cowboys use to tie cattle. It was a sure bet that, if a steer can't break free from them, Pete sure as hell wouldn't.

About ten feet off to his right and facing him lay the bodies of Reynolds and Jenkins. Evans awoke to find ants crawling on his face and chest.

After only a second or two, he started yapping.

"What's going on? Get me outta here. Untie me." He wasn't screaming yet, that came later. For now he was just jittery.

As for me, I couldn't have been more relaxed. The hour I'd spent whittling in the shade of that tree had a nice calming effect, until Evans woke up, that is. After that he never shut up, whining the whole time. I let him go on for a while. Before I really went to work on him, I thought I'd give him a chance to confess on his own.

"Well, Pete," I said quietly. "Seems like you three were involved in a little rustling a short time back. Why don't you tell me all about it. Start with where the herd is now, who's behind it, and finish with who ambushed that scout just before the raid."

"I don't know what you're talkin' about," he said. "Any horses got stole warn't by me. Maybe it was those two." He nodded toward the bodies. "Hell, I just met them, don't even know 'em that good."

"Then how'd you know I was talking about horses? I didn't mention it. Most folks around here would have thought I meant a herd of cattle."

"Uh, I just guessed," he answered unconvincingly.

I decided to speed things up a little. Taking out my Bowie knife, I bent over quickly and slashed his forearm.

"Damn, what's that for?" he screamed.

"Ants love fresh blood. Ever see them after they finish with a body, Pete? Isn't a pretty sight. And in case you're wondering why you're itching so much, you happen to be lying over an ant hill. It's a well-known Apache cure for lyin' and thievin'."

"Get me outta here. I swear I didn't rob those Mexes." More ants began crawling around on his face, and he was struggling hard against his straps.

"Whoa, wrong answer, hoss. I didn't say anything about who the herd belonged to. But now that you mention it, Pete, there is a whole pack of angry Mexican *vaqueros* after my hide. Seems they wrongly think I had something to do with them losing their herd. So you see I don't have a whole lot of time to waste."

I took a small piece of wood and measured it against his eyelids.

"What the hell you doing now? Are you loco? I can't help you, honest." Sweat poured down his forehead, stinging his eyes.

"I'm gonna prop your eyelids open with these here pieces of wood, like the Apaches do. I'm sure you can figure it out. With the sun as hot as it is, shouldn't take more than an hour or two for you to go blind. You know, Pete, you might prefer to talk. Otherwise, I get to find out which drives a man crazy first, having his eyes burned out by the sun or being slowly eaten alive by ants. You mentioned a name during our card game. Davies, I think it was. Why don't you start there." I snapped a piece of wood for effect and he immediately began screaming.

"You're right . . . Davies hired us, he hired the three of us. God, get these ants off of me."

"Go on," I said quietly.

"Comes from California, but he already knew all about that herd. Wants to take some fellow's ranch away from him back home, and figured, if those horses ever got through to be sold, it would spoil things for him. So Davies had the herd rustled. His men are driving it west so he can sell the horses himself. Changed the brand, too. The three of us dropped out after the first part of the job was done 'cause Reynolds didn't want to ride all the way back to California."

"What did they change the brand to?" I asked.

"Four Box. Used a runnin' wire to close off the old brand."

That would be simple enough. With a hot wire you could close the top and bottom of the H and the side of the E to make two double boxes. Hence, the 4 Box brand.

"How'd he know when the herd was coming?"

"Someone tipped him . . . telegraph, I think . . . but I swear I don't know who. Now untie me!"

I ignored his pleas. "Another thing. There was a man bushwhacked just before your gang hit the herd. Who did it?"

"It must have been Pierce. Luke Pierce. Reynold's knew him from sometime back, they rode together I think. He's Davies's right-hand man now. All I knows is Pierce rode out ahead, and then came back later riding a different horse."

"A Morgan bay?"

"Think so. Yeah, that's right."

"How do I recognize this Pierce fellow?" I asked.

"Sandy hair and moustache. Tall . . . about your height and size. Always wears two pistols butt forward. You know, crossdraw style."

No wonder the Hernandez outfit thought me guilty! After convincing them to change directions, I'd disappeared, leaving them to face an ambush led by someone riding my horse. On top of that, with a hat and bandanna mask to hide his face, Pierce apparently could have easily been mistaken for me.

I got up and walked over to my horse, having already tied the others together.

"Hey, what about me?" Evans screamed.

"What about you?" I said as I saddled up.

"God, don't leave me here. I can't stand it."

He was shaking his head frantically back and forth.

I laughed to myself a little before slowly answering. If he had only shut up and thought about it a while he'd have figured out something was wrong. Not enough ants for one thing.

"See, Pete, that ant hill you've been lying on's been dead for quite some time. I just brought a few ants from over yonder to keep you company."

"But you're goin' to leave me staked out here! I'll die anyway."

"You worry too much. Just keep on struggling and those pegs ought to work loose in a couple of hours. It'll be dark in an hour or so, so you won't really burn much. After that, I suggest you bury your friends with that shovel over there." I was actually enjoying this part.

"What about my cayuse?" he asked.

I tossed a half empty canteen on the ground.

"The horses come with me. Might make up for the ones you stole. Besides, walking ought to do you some good. You should make it into town in a couple of days. After that leave the territory, 'cause I swear the next time we meet I won't be so generous," I said, mounting the roan.

"What if you're wrong about these stakes comin' loose?" he shouted.

"In that case," I said, turning the horses around, "Jenkins and Reynolds will have a third for poker. In hell."

I rode out, leaving Evans lying there, screaming back at me, but I wasn't listening. My mind was focused instead on someone named Luke Pierce. It now appeared I had more than one account to settle with the man.

Chapter Fourteen

Elijah leaned his pitchfork against the barn wall and eyed the horses I was leading.

"Ah see those saddle bums caught up with you. Or was it visy versy?"

"A little of both," I replied. "One thing's for sure, they won't be needing these ponies any longer," I added.

"Figured that much when Ah seed you ride in," he said, wiping his forehead with the back of his hand.

"Look, I'm going to be leaving again, but this time I've got a long way to go, so I'll be needing more supplies. Suppose I could get a fair price for these two horses?" I asked.

"Depends on what you consider a fair price."

"All I need is a change of clothes, some more ammunition, and enough grub to get me where I'm going. Might even check out that bathhouse you mentioned before."

"Well, seein' as how mah brother-in-law runs the mercantile, Ah reckon we can strike a deal. What about the other one?" he asked, pointing to the chestnut gelding with the EH brand.

"Just leave him in the corral and feed him. I expect some boys from that same brand will be along soon to claim him," I said.

"Iffen they ain't friends o' yorn, you might want to reconsider takin' time fer that bath," he said knowingly.

"Why's that?" I asked.

"Already been here. About three hours after you rode out, a group o' Mexes rode in. Ah couldn't help noticin' but they was ridin' that same EH brand you are. Ain't none o' mah business, but those boys kept askin' 'bout someone who kinda fits your general description. 'Course, Ah don't savvy none o' that *mejicano palaber,* but Ah got the dee-stinct impression that whoever the fellow is that they's a-lookin' fer, he ain't gonna be none too happy when they catch up with him."

I glanced quickly back over my shoulder. "You tell 'em where I went?"

"Iffen Ah had, they'd 'a' found you by now. Nope, they didn't offer me nothin' fer mah trouble like you did, and Ah always figured a businessman ought to take care of his good payin' cash customers first. Besides, maybe you'll take that into account when we agree on the final price for these cayuses," he said, grinning.

"You just saved yourself a lot of money, friend. Know where these *vaqueros* might be right about now?"

"Oh, Ah figure they still ought to be headin' on north. Guess Ah kinda intimated it was a good idea. Ah remembered how you rode out o' here to the west, by the way."

"Much obliged. But with no trail to follow, they might backtrack any time, right?" I looked around again apprehensively.

"Might at that," he said. "But then again, that

stretch is so bad iffen they was a-lookin' fer sign, and iffen they wanted to find someone real bad like, they prob'ly wouldn't stop until they hit the nearest water hole. That's the only way they'd be sure, and it's a good two days ride from here. 'Course, it's none o' mah business," he continued on, "but iffen you were the feller they's a-lookin' fer, Ah figure you got about a full day or so, afore they git back."

"Hadn't counted on them finding me so soon," I said. "Thanks again for the help."

Elijah just nodded back at me.

"Look, when they come back this time, don't take any chances, just tell them straight out where I went," I warned.

"Truth is there ain't a-gonna be no next time. When that outfit comes back, Ah don't plan on bein' around to answer any more questions. Especially not after what they done to the Golden Goose."

"How's that?" I asked.

"After they left here, they headed straight fer the saloon. Most folks usually do."

"So what happened?"

"Ah followed them down there an' saw the whole thing. They all went in, peaceful enough like, and ordered beers and a few tequilas. The bartender served them all right, but then this one feller, name o' Morton, he don't cotton to Mexes much, and starts givin' 'em a hard time. Called 'em a bunch of stinkin' beaners and let on that the folks in the bar don't want their kind around. Well, sir, one of them Mexes starts to object, but Morton, he's kind of a big feller, he just shoves him backward and reaches behind the bar for a sawed-off shotgun that's kept there. Then he sets it on the bar top and starts talkin big to his friends, you know, braggin' a lot. Ah could tell those Mexes was hot, but this other feller with a scar on his face, guess he's the boss, he sort o' holds up his hand to stop them from startin' a fight."

"That would be their ramrod, Chavez," I offered.

"Iffen you say so. Anyway, this Chavez feller, he takes out a ceegar from his shirt pocket and lights up. Then he motions to the barkeep to buy this Morton feller a drink. Next this other Mex translates for him that they ain't a gonna fight with 'em. Says they's just passin' through and ain't lookin' fer no trouble."

"I assume it didn't help?"

"Hell, no. This Morton, he just laughs, and starts bragging again to his friends about how many Mexican whores he's had. Then he and some o' his pals order all the Mexes out of the place."

"And they just took that?" I asked surprised.

"Well, Ah'll tell you. This Chavez feller shrugs his shoulders, and then turns to leave. But, see, he stops first to put out his cigar on the bar."

"Then what happened?" I asked. Chavez was hardly the mild-mannered type.

"Oh, he put the cigar out all right. But as it turns out, he ground it right into the back of Morton's hand. Well, Ah'll tell you, that man yelped loud enough to wake the dead, and pulls up his hand in pain. Next thing ya know this Chavez feller grabs up the shotgun and clouts him right across the nose with it. Man, that Morton went down like he was pole-axed. After that the rest of them started swinging at anyone in sight. And them Mexes, they got this one big bald feller."

"Chango," I said, nodding.

"Whatever. Anyway, he grabs this one cowboy up over his head and throws him clear through the gambling wheel like he was a dart. Went right through the middle, flying headfirst. When the bodies started sailin' through the windows is when Ah skedaddled out of there. Last Ah heard every table was broke, two cowboys lost an ear, and the barkeep got part o' his nose bit off. One cowboy 'parently pulled a gun. They found him later under a table, with three holes in him, two in the chest and one in the gut. Right here." He pointed to his belly, indicating the precise spot.

"Any of them *mejicanos* hurt?" I asked.

"Saw 'im ride out right afterwards. Couple of bloody noses and one fellow was cut a little on the arm, but nothing serious. Leastwise nothing Ah could see."

"How many riders were there?" I asked.

"About twenty or so, Ah reckon."

"Seems they're madder than I thought, to have brought that many."

"Son, mad don't touch it. Just ask the fellers at the Golden Goose, or what's left of it," he said.

"Any place left in town to get a drink now?" I asked.

"Yeah, but Ah'd have to show you," he answered, licking his lips in anticipation.

"All right, you do that, and I'll spring for the drinks." I laughed. "And then we can talk to your brother-in-law about those supplies."

When we walked past what remained of the

Golden Goose, I could see that Elijah hadn't exaggerated. After that I was more determined than ever not to let those *vaqueros* catch up with me until I had a chance to find the herd and square things.

Chapter Fifteen

I left Gila City at first light, aiming for Fort Yuma.

I rode hard and fast, trying to put as much distance between myself and the *vaqueros* as possible. This time I made no effort to cover my trail, since after a day or two it would be obvious to everyone where I was going.

A week later I arrived at the Butterfield stage way station. It was the logical place to stop and rest, the food was good, and they didn't water their drinks. I had hoped finally to clean up some before moving into California, but as usual it was not meant to be.

After tending to the roan, I went into the station house. Since I'd run out of bacon three days earlier, visions of a hot steak, mashed potatoes, and biscuits flashed briefly through my mind. It was only briefly, though, for, as soon as I opened the door, the commotion inside wiped away any hope of a nice quiet meal.

Inside eight heavily built drovers had a lone black cowboy trapped in a corner and were preparing to beat him up. One of the men had a bottle in his hand and was raising it to strike just as I entered. For some reason it didn't surprise me one bit to find Sonora Mason on the receiving end, staring back at me from the corner. For the time being lunch would have to wait.

"'Afternoon, gents," I said as loudly and forcefully as I could. "Just goin' over to the bar here. Don't mind me. I'm not lookin' to interfere with your fun."

Caught off guard by my unexpected entrance, they all turned toward me and hesitated.

"By the way, just what is going on here anyway?" I asked.

"We're about to brain us a smart-mouthed nigger," replied the one brandishing the bottle. He was a fat, bearded lout missing all his front teeth. He wore an old buffalo-hide vest and a ten-gallon black hat with the brim turned up. "Any problem with that, stranger?" he asked threateningly.

"Why would anyone have a problem with that?" I asked innocently. "Besides, anyone can see he's the type that's probably getting what he deserves," I added. "Just look at those shifty eyes of his."

Sonora caught my wink after they turned back to him.

"What's that you say? Hey, you want to buy into this, too, asshole, or you just some big-mouth pansy with no stones to back it up?" Mason yelled across at me.

"Well, now. . . . Boy!" I shouted angrily. "Just who the hell do you think you are, talking to me that way?" I spoke loudly, hoping further to distract the others. Stepping quickly away from the bar, I shoved my way through the crowd until I faced Mason, directly alongside the drover with the bottle.

"You know," I said turning to Buffalo Vest. "There's only one thing I hate worse than an uppity nigger."

"Yeah?" he asked anticipating the joke. "What's that?"

"Having to fight a bunch of ignorant cowpunchers, instead of eating lunch!" My right elbow crashed into the side of his head. It wasn't exactly the answer he'd expected.

The next ten minutes still remain something of a blur. I vaguely remember Mason kicking the nearest drover in the knee, and then backhanding him as he doubled over in pain. I ducked low under a chair that was swung at my head by a bald type in an old soldier shirt. He was wearing tied down bat chaps that flared out widely at the bottom, so I grabbed for the chaps near his ankles, and then pulled as hard as I could while straightening back up. He was thrown backward off his feet, slammed through a table, and hit the floor flat on his back.

Someone cuffed me behind the left ear hard enough to knock me forward into Mason. He stopped my fall, but, as I began to recover, he suddenly shoved me hard on the shoulders, causing me to drop back down again. Another drover coming up behind me ran smack into Sonora's fist as Mason slugged right over my head directly into his oncoming face. The drover fell over backward like someone who'd just run into a wall.

I turned around and side-by-side the two of us rushed into the remaining four. When it was all over, my knuckles were swollen, my lower lip split, and my left ear was bleeding. Sonora was holding his left shoulder where a broken bottle had slashed him and had another gash over his right elbow. The others looked a hell of a lot worse.

We supported ourselves on what was left of the bar as I reached over, searching for a bottle.

"Didn't expect to bump into you," Sonora said somewhat matter-of-factly.

"Oh, don't mention it. You're welcome. Nice to see you again, too," I said, gasping for breath. He just nodded back at me. "Care for some o' this tarantula juice?" I asked. My head hurt like hell.

"Don't mind if I do," he replied.

I poured him a long one, and then took a swig from the bottle. The effect of the alcohol on my split lip sent sparks flying through my body and right down to my boots.

"Best be gettin' outta here afore they wake up," he suggested.

I wasn't about to disagree.

We decided to make a quick exit after first grabbing some supplies from the station's storeroom. Mason caught me tossing some money on one of the shelves and laughed at me.

"Momma brought her boy up real proper, I see."

"Hey, get off my back, would ya. I got enough people after me as is without getting the stage line detectives involved."

"You being chased? That's a new one."

"Long story, I'll tell you about it later."

As we were leaving the station, Buffalo Vest groaned and started to sit up. Mason simply kicked him in the face as he stepped over him. The last thing I remember as we walked out the door was the sound of his head hitting the floor with a loud *thud*.

That night we camped about twenty miles west. The cut on Sonora's shoulder looked pretty bad so I offered to fix it.

"Got anything to work with?" I asked.

"Check my *mochila*, back of the saddle. Should be a sewing kit in there." I looked in his saddle-bag and found some old buttons and a couple of needles, but no thread.

"Looks like I'm going to have to improvise a might," I said, walking back to his horse. I began pulling tail hair. Then I poured a little of the whiskey into a cup, dropping in both the needle and horse hair. I tossed Sonora the bottle. "Here, wash that wound with this."

He looked at me apprehensively while removing his shirt. "You sure you know how to do this?" He grimaced as the alcohol ran over the cut on his shoulder.

"Don't worry, I learned how from my uncle Zeke. He's a leathersmith back home, and, judging from the look of this hide of yours, it shouldn't be much different from the leather we worked on." I removed the needle and hair from the whiskey cup.

"Just you remember this hide is my skin. It ain't no saddle, you know."

"'Course not," I replied, threading the needle. "A good saddle's worth a whole lot more."

"Very funny." He flinched as I began to sew, but I had to hand it to him again. It took a long time to get that wound stitched up, and it had to hurt, but he didn't complain once; he just sat there and took it in stride.

When I finished, I poured some more whiskey over the wound and bandaged it with an extra shirt I'd found in his *mochila*.

"You know, I'm getting a little tired of nursemaiding injured renegades all the time," I joked.

"Didn't nobody ask you to jump in," he replied.

"That all the thanks I get for saving your sorry ass?"

"Hell, there was only eight of them. Could've handled things myself."

"Well, I'll remember that the next time around."

"*Hombre,* I don't know about you, but I hope there won't be a next time." He started laughing, and I joined in.

"Shoulder or no shoulder, you get to cook dinner tonight," I said, throwing more wood on the fire. "What's in those cans, anyway?"

Mason eyed the supplies carefully. "You're in luck. We have a wide selection. Canned tomatoes and beans or canned beans and tomatoes."

"I'll have the beans and tomatoes," I sighed.

"Good choice. As it turns out, they're my specialty."

"Didn't expect to find you in these parts. Last I heard you were down around Zacatecas," I said.

"My friends were for a while, but I had some personal business to attend to at the fort."

"Anything to do with those drovers?" I asked.

"Nope. They was just a few mule heads that didn't want to drink while there was a gentleman of color in the establishment."

"Some folks are just downright impolite," I replied.

"Truth is, I'm visiting a friend of mine, a sergeant with the Tenth Cavalry."

"The buffalo soldiers? I didn't think they were posted at Yuma."

"They're not," he replied. "But my friend is with a special troop on detached duty."

"Must be quite a friend for you to come this far out of your way just to say hello."

"He is. His name's Freeman, Nathaniel Freeman. After Pa escaped from the plantation he was slavin' on, Nate helped him make his way into Mexico where he finally met my mama. Nate was real kind to me after they both died."

"Sounds like a good man. So how come you didn't end up joining the Army like him?" I asked.

Sonora ladled a thick mess of overcooked beans into my tin. As they dripped down onto the plate, he looked up at me and smiled.

"*Hombre,* no way! Not for me. Have you ever tasted how bad that Army cookin' is?"

I looked down at the glob on my plate, and then back up at him. "Of course," I replied. "I understand . . . completely."

Chapter Sixteen

During the ride to the fort the next day Sonora got to philosophizing on one of his favorite subjects, namely those who wanted to make him conform to their way of doing things.

"Ever notice how some folks are always tryin' to tell you how to act?" he asked.

"Sure, there's always someone like that around, so?"

"Well, it just seems to me that we was a country supposed to be formed by runaway folk, like them pilgrims. They just wanted to be left alone, ya know. Nowadays it seems like we got more political parties and do-gooder temperance groups telling us what to do, than we got people actually doin' it. Hell, I even heard there's some place in Kansas what won't let you carry a gun in town. You hear about that?" he asked.

"Yeah, I did. They call it a deadline. Anyone passing over it has to check his guns with the sheriff or he gets arrested."

"So what you think about that," he asked.

"Well, I'll tell you. My uncle Zeke used to be in the military for a while and studied a little law. According to him, we all got individual rights, you know, ones no one can take away. My uncle said that somewhere in the Constitution, or the

Bill of Rights, or something, it says we all got a right to keep and bear arms."

"Right, but what about those badges what try to take them away?"

"Uncle Zeke said there's a part in there to protect us against a corrupt government. Funny thing, but he says the Constitution don't actually grant rights . . . we already have them . . . it just spells them out clearly. Seems when the Constitution was written and they got to talkin' about folks protectin' themselves, they used a very specific word . . . infringement."

" 'Fringement? What's that?"

"Zeke says it means the government can't mess with your right to carry. 'The right to bear arms shall not be infringed,' " I quoted.

"Well, some folk say that you can keep your gun, but just can't wear it. Says it's better for the town," he pointed out.

"I once asked my uncle a similar question. He says the founding fathers didn't set things up so our rights could be tromped on in the name of a supposed greater good for the majority. See if it's an individual right, like the right to free speech or to protect your family or home, it's still a right, regardless what the local star says. Funny thing, I hear the bank in that town you mentioned has already been robbed four times, and the sheriff never caught any of the robbers."

"That figures," Sonora remarked.

"Well, my point is in a town just across the state line they had a couple of stick-ups, but the townsfolk were all armed. The robbers didn't even clear the main street before being caught."

"Makes sense," Sonora agreed. "You know

someone's got a gun an' another ain't, you gonna rob the one what ain't."

"Bet you dollars to donuts those that obey the deadline are all law-abiding citizens. You know . . . the kind you wouldn't have to worry about anyway."

"'Course they is. Hell, man, why do you think they call them outlaws, 'cause they don't obey the law."

"Well, someday I hope to hang my gun up, Sonora. But rest assured, when I do, it will still be hanging within reach."

"You bet. By the way, you know that cayuse o' yours is favoring his leg?" he added.

"I know. He's been a little off all morning. Right front, I think."

"Best have it looked at when we get to the fort."

"I will. How far you figure we still got to go?"

Sonora squinted a little and rubbed his eyes. "Oh, about another two hours, Ah reckon."

He was right as usual, almost to the minute. As we rode through the gate, a sentry quickly looked us over and waved us by. Sonora stopped to ask the private about his sergeant friend.

"Sorry," the trooper replied. "I'm new on the post, don't know everyone yet. You might ask over at the sutler's store, though. By the way, your friend's horse seems to be favoring his leg."

"We know," I answered. "You suppose someone here might be able to check him out?"

"That I can help you with. Doctor Chapman's our vet'nry, and a good one to boot. Anyone can put a horse right, he can."

"Thanks," I replied as he pointed the way for us.

We looked for Dr. Chapman as instructed in

the main horse barn. A long white jacket hanging on a nail identified the stall where we found him examining a large black gelding. The veterinarian was a tall, solidly built man with a full beard that was starting to gray. He wore a long church bell-shaped stethoscope around his neck, had his sleeves rolled up, and was using a large magnifying glass to inspect a horse's right eye. A shorter, slightly balding trooper was busy writing something down in a small notebook while the doctor dictated.

". . . small nebula in the temporal quadrant of the right eye and an active corneal ulceration in same location on the left. Eyelids, sclera, and pupillary reflex appear normal. Got all that, Corporal?"

"Excuse me," Sonora said, interrupting the two. "You the horse doctor here?"

"Veterinary surgeon," he responded, sharply correcting Mason.

"What's the difference?" chided Sonora.

"Well, let's see . . . captain's bars, a six month sabbatical in Lyons, France, eleven-hour shifts tending the unit's mounts, public health duties, plus I get to keep the colonel's dog free of ticks. All that for the generous sum of sixty-five dollars per month."

"My horse's favoring his front leg some," I said more respectfully. "I'd appreciate it, if you'd glance at it. Couldn't find anything obvious myself."

"You're new around here," the corporal said, more a statement than a question.

"Just rode in," I replied.

"You boys on the Army payroll? Scouts?" he asked.

"Not presently."

"Jus' passin' through," added Mason rather curtly.

"Private consult will cost you extra. Ten dollars ought to do, I expect," Dr. Chapman said rather seriously.

"What?" I exclaimed, somewhat shocked at the price.

"What did I tell you, Corporal. Folks'll think nothing of paying a barkeep extra for a drink, or for a carpenter to fix a drawer, but they'll begrudge a professional his consultation fee every time. Even after four years of advanced schoolin'." Turning to face me, he smiled and added: "Just funnin' with you, son. You see, for some strange reason, the corporal here wants to apprentice with me. Actually, the Army pays my keep. I'll be glad to have a look-see." Then, turning to Sonora, he added: "After all, we've only a couple hundred horses to treat on the post. Don't reckon one more will kill me."

Sonora didn't see it, but I caught the wink he threw to the corporal, who rolled his eyes and mumbled something I didn't quite catch.

"I'll get the hoof testers, sir," he said to the veterinarian. Turning back to me, the corporal indicated a spot in the barn's center aisle.

I led the roan over and replaced his bridle with the halter the corporal offered me. Then I crossed-tied the roan.

"He's a little feisty today," I warned.

"Corporal, if you'd be so kind," Dr. Chapman said, nodding.

"Yes, sir," the corporal answered, taking out a twitch made of a loop of short chain attached to the top end of an axe handle.

The corporal placed his hand through the chain and calmly walked up to the roan sideways, keeping the twitch hidden behind his leg and out of the horse's sight. He slowly reached up and then quickly grabbed the horse's upper lip, withdrawing his hand and firmly pulling the lip through the chain loop. Before the roan had a chance to react, the corporal turned the axe handle several times, screwing the chain down onto the lip.

When a cayuse has its lip all twisted like that, it effectively immobilizes it. A twitch works better than trying to hang on to a lip by hand, although some of the stronger *vaqueros* achieve the same effect by twisting an ear, or with a Mexican twitch, which they perform by simply grabbing a large fold on the side of a horse's neck with their bare hands and rolling the skin up tightly. If a man's strong enough, sometimes he can hold on this way long enough for the horse to be shod, or for minor surgeries to be performed.

Someone who really wants to gain control, however, will use a rope or chain twitch because it applies more squeeze and allows for better leverage over the horse. Sure enough, that roan stood as still for the veterinary as a stopped clock.

The corporal then wrapped the halter's lead rope around the twitch's handle and held it tightly with both hands.

"Prevents the handle from flying up and clouting you in the face when the horse shakes his head," Dr. Chapman explained.

The fact that the corporal was missing several teeth indicated to me that he probably learned that trick from personal experience.

"Not likely to move much with that thing cuttin' into his lip so hard," muttered Sonora.

"The corporal knows his job, all right. This won't hurt him in the least," commented Dr. Chapman after overhearing Mason's remark. He bent over and began to run his hands down the horse's legs, one at a time.

"Seems to favor the front leg," I offered.

"Uhn-huh. Right front. Saw the way he throws his head up slightly as he walked in. Takes the weight off the bad leg. Best to check them all, though."

"Couldn't find any cracks or stones when we looked. Suppose he's foundering?" Sonora asked the veterinarian as he started his exam.

"Well, I'll tell you," Dr. Chapman answered, looking over his shoulder, still bent over with the horse's leg cupped in his hands. "I'm pretty good at these things, but, you know, I've never yet figured out a way to make a correct diagnosis *before* I've had a chance to examine the patient."

He was smiling at Sonora when he said it, but his message came across clear enough.

"Right you are, Doc," Sonora replied. "I'll just let you get on with it."

Captain Chapman proceeded to pull the shoe and, with a curved knife he snatched from his rear pocket, trim away some of the tissue from around the frog and sole.

"Hoof testers, Corporal."

The testers were actually large round pincers used to apply pressure around the edges and bottom of the hoof. The roan flinched a time or two before the veterinarian finished his exam.

"You're lucky," Dr. Chapman said, washing his

hands off in a nearby water bucket. "Seems to be just a stone bruise. No sign of problems with the navicular bone and no sign of rot."

"Any recommendations?" I asked, somewhat relieved.

"Take him next door to Sergeant Emerson. I'll write you up some instructions to give him," he said, taking the notebook from the corporal. "Not that he'll follow them," I overheard his mumble. "I want him to build up the shoe a little and cut a sole pad to go under the shoe. It ought to protect the sole long enough to heal while still allowing you to ride him." The captain shook his head. "That is if the good sergeant doesn't lame him in the process."

"A little heavy-handed, is he?" I asked, wishing Chango were around to do the job.

"I've seen apes in a zoo with a softer touch. 'Course, you understand that if this were to get back to the sergeant, I'd deny ever having said the like."

Considering the size of most farriers I'd met, I could fully appreciate his position.

"Don't leave that pad on longer than a month," he added. "Tends to soften things up, and, if you aren't careful, the sole will get a little mucky."

I thanked the captain and, remembering his earlier comments, offered to pay something for his extra effort. He just waved it away.

The corporal untied the roan, and then Sonora and I headed next door to look for the troop's farrier.

"Orders from the captain, eh? As if I didn't have enough to do already." Sergeant Emerson apparently wasn't in the best of moods.

"Yes, sir," I answered.

"Don't sir me. I ain't no officer, I work for a living," he snapped.

"Right."

"And I suppose you're in a hurry."

This time it was Sonora who answered. "That's right. The colonel needs us to do some scoutin' for him. And he said the sooner the better."

I shot him a quick look, but Sonora's expression was dead pan.

"Christ, that's all I need." The sergeant had been working on a large gray jenny. He dropped the hoof and tossed the shoe he had pulled into a wooden box in the corner.

Sergeant Emerson was a dark-haired, husky sort, about thirty years of age, which I roughly estimated to be the amount of time passed since he last changed his uniform. It was hard to believe, but he actually smelled worse than the barn he worked in. The remnants of a fat cigar whose flame had long gone out clung to his lips, even when he spoke.

We tied up the roan and the sergeant bent over to examine his feet. "The shoes in back look all right. I'll just replace the ones up front the good doctor saw fit to pull."

"You know, the vet suggested we fill in the front hoofs and have a pad put on," I added.

"I can read," he growled. "Christ, it turns out everythin' that quack looks at either needs corrective shoes or some special damn' pad." He selected a rasp out of another box, and spit on it. As he began to trim the hoof, the sergeant shook his head at us.

"File and shape the hoof. Build the shoe up.

Huh! Probably just a damned nail abscess. You drive one in too deep or screw up the angle and you lame the horse sure as I'm standing here. Probably the last smith's fault."

Knowing the type of work Chango Lopez did, I doubted that was the case, but I wasn't about to argue the point. Like Pa always said, when you wrestle with pigs, you both get dirty, but only the pig enjoys it.

"Well, just the same, I wouldn't want to piss off the captain, not to mention the colonel," I added, remembering the sergeant's reaction when Mason first mentioned him.

"By the way, you know a master sergeant by the name of Freeman?" I asked. "Nathaniel."

Emerson began pounding out a shoe on his anvil. He paused to look up at me before answering.

"Nigger sergeant from that unit what came in with the inspector? What about him?" he asked, returning to his work.

It was as if he was totally ignoring Sonora's presence. I saw Mason's face begin to tense as he started past me angrily; I shot my arm out sideways, palm against his chest.

"He ain't worth it, *hombre,*" I whispered. "No sense causing problems before you've found your friend. We're almost done. Just let him finish and we're outta here."

Sonora just stared at me. His eyes were empty and his jaw locked, but reluctantly he nodded back.

I turned to the sergeant. "Yeah, that's the one. Know where we can find him?"

"Probably with the rest o' his kind. They got a few tents staked out back of the fort." He pointed his hammer to indicate the direction. "No sense letting them stay inside with the decent folk," he added snidely.

Mason, I'd noticed, had quietly walked to the far side of the barn and was now leaning against a wooden stall post while we waited.

Sergeant Emerson hammered the last of the horseshoe nails, prying back the exposed ends till they broke off. He then smoothed the whole affair with another rasp, repeating his spitting routine.

"That oughter do 'er," he said. "Leastwise the shoes are on and the damn' hoof 's padded. Oh, and don't forget to mention that to the colonel. Don't want him on my case for not finishing B Troop on time."

"Oh, I'm sure the colonel will hear of it, all right," I said. "Come on, Sonora, we're through here."

The sergeant was standing just behind the roan when I began to untie the harness. Mason had come up on the horse's left side while I was replacing the bridle.

"Thank you, Sergeant," he said unexpectedly. "We do 'preciate it. This'n here's mah pahtnahs best friend. Ain't that right?" Sonora's accent had suddenly grown unusually thick. Surprised, I looked back at him dumbly. "Yes-siree, he's a great hoss. A mite feisty, though." With that he gave the roan a firm slap on the rump. The gelding let out a loud whinny and jumped off its rear legs, mule-kicking straight back. Those big rear legs caught the blacksmith just above the belt, knocking him at least four feet backward. Emerson was out for the count.

"Christ!" I exclaimed, trying to calm the horse down.

"*Hmmm.* Hoss must not like white-assed sergeants very much," Sonora said, shrugging his shoulders. As he turned around, I noticed something fall from his hand. "Nigger sergeant, my ass," Sonora remarked, cussing back at the now unconscious blacksmith. "Nate Freeman craps better than the likes of him," he added, walking out the door.

The roan's sudden reaction had come as quite a surprise until I stopped near the object Sonora had dropped, bent over, and picked it up. What I found turned out to be a sharpened two inch long wooden splinter!

Chapter Seventeen

Although the entrance to Yuma had a manned wall around its gate, the rest of the fort was actually more like a series of several connecting buildings than a closed-in four-walled structure.

In order to get to the tented area where Sergeant Freeman's unit was bivouacked we had to cross part of the drill field and then pass between the enlisted men's barracks and the quartermaster's office.

After leaving the stable, I tethered the roan to the nearest hitching post and accompanied Sonora Mason as he started out across the field in search of his friend. Off to the right a firearms instructor was drilling a platoon of new recruits.

"The standard U.S. Army cavalry issue shoulder arm is the Springfield Armory modified breechloading Trapdoor model carbine," we overheard him lecture the men. I was already familiar with the rifle version. Although the .50–70 caliber was a strong cartridge, and even though the rifle had fairly good long-range accuracy, I was disappointed when the Army adopted it as their standard for infantry issue. The rifle was heavy, and its long bayonet worthless for Western fighting. The carbine version was an even worse choice for the cavalry.

We paused to watch the drill.

"What's your opinion of the standard Army issue shoulder arm, Sonora?" I asked, watching the men struggle with the manual of arms.

"Some politician sure padded his nest with that one. You know damn' well that group up north with Forsythe would never have survived the Beecher's Island attack if they'd had these single-shot Springfields. Their Spencers was what saved their asses, and then the Army goes and trades 'em away."

I agreed. Everyone knew the details of the battle for Beecher's Island. Major George A. Forsythe had been detailed by General Sheridan to lead a small force of fifty men in order to draw out the Sioux and Cheyennes, who had been raiding stage and telegraph stations.

On September 16, 1868 Forsythe made camp in the valley of the Arikaree River, mistakenly believing that he had arrived undetected. At dawn the next day 600 Sioux, Cheyennes, and Arapahos led by Roman Nose moved in to attack. Fortunately for the cavalrymen some overeager young braves tried to stampede the Army's horses first. Their war cries alerted Forsythe who managed to drive off the raiders and withdraw his force across the river and onto a small island before the main body of Indians attacked.

Forsythe's men brought their mounts around into a circle and tied them to bushes, forming a tight barrier. The island was an ideal defensive position, but what really saved Forsythe, who was outnumbered more than twelve to one, was the fact that every man carried a Spencer repeating rifle with 140 rounds and Colt Army revolver with another 100 or so rounds. Four Army pack mules carried another 4,000 extra shells for the rifles.

Time and time again the Indian charges were broken by volleys from the trooper's Spencer rifles, fully loaded with six in the magazine, and one in the chamber.

Under siege for over a week the men huddled in rifle pits dug with tin plates and hunting knives. Major Forsythe was wounded on the first day, but his courage continued to inspire his men. By the fourth day he had been hit twice more and his second-in-command, Lieutenant Frederick Beecher, for whom the island was eventually named, had been killed.

Roman Nose was a fearless leader and relentlessly continued the onslaught, leading one of the largest charges himself. Since they had little time to reload, Forsythe held his fire, ordering his men to shoot in volleys. The troopers were ordered to hold fire until the redskins were a mere fifty yards away. But those Spencers held seven rounds apiece, and, when they finally cut loose, wave after wave of Indians fell to its devastating firepower.

When the fifth wave collapsed, Roman Nose managed once again to rally his braves, and charged a sixth time. With only two more rounds left, the troopers fired and Roman Nose was hit point-blank, knocking him off his horse and into the shallow waters. The charge faltered, the Indians demoralized.

By the time the Army's relief column finally arrived, what was left of Forsythe's men had been reduced to eating the horses that had died during the fighting.

Cavalrymen everywhere were grateful for the extra firepower offered by the Spencer rifle, but the Army, with its usual logic, decided to replace it with the single-shot Springfield.

"Ever seen what happens to a Trapdoor that's been fired a lot?" I asked Sonora. "The barrel heats up and the cartridges swell and stick in the breech. Got to pry 'em out with a pocket knife," I said.

Sonora nodded his head. "Single-shot's a great idea for cavalry. Reloading one's real easy, especially when you're galloping at the enemy," he added sarcastically.

"Heard they were considering the Remington Rolling Block for a while," I commented.

"Never had a chance," he replied. "Sure, it's a better rifle, so's the Sharps for that matter. But it's a lot easier for the government to retool old rifles and pocket the difference. Never mind the men what's got to use 'em."

The drill continued as we walked past.

"You'll get a full sixty rounds a month for target practice, so make 'em count." The instructor sounded less than convincing that it would be enough.

We passed through the buildings and onto an open field in back of the fort, where we found a dozen or more two-man pup tents staked out in equal columns. Standing out in front of them, talking to a couple of his men was a sergeant who, judging from Sonora's description, had to be the man we were looking for.

Sonora Mason could hardly be described as soft, yet here he was hugging his friend and thumping his back, happy as a kid at Christmas. The fact that Sergeant Freeman was a good man was immediately obvious to me, but at the present time he was also an embarrassed one.

"Let me go, ya big idiot, afore you crack a rib," he gasped.

"Damn it's good to see you, Nate."

"Sure it is, kid, but Ah'm on duty. Army cain't have its noncoms going 'round huggin' other men. 'Specially not someone ugly as y'all." He laughed.

Sergeant Nathaniel Freeman was a man of average height, but solidly built. His short-cropped, curly gray hair was thinning, and his face wrinkled, but he walked tall and his uniform was sharp, unusually so for a Southwestern post.

"Glad ya got mah letter, but Ah didn't expect ya'd come all this way. Whose the galoot with y'all?" he asked, glancing my way.

"Don't get the wrong idea, Nate. He's white, oversized, and he'll talk your ear off given half a chance, but he's a friend of sorts," Sonora said, looking over at me.

"Thanks a lot, Sonora" I said. "Don't bust a cinch loadin' on all that praise."

"Sonora?" The sergeant looked puzzled. "That's what you callin' yourself now, Isiquiel?"

"Isiquiel?" I laughed. "You've got to be kidding."

"Never you mind," he growled. "And you just better keep it to yourself," he added.

"Sure thing. I can keep a secret as well as the next man . . . Isiquiel."

Before he had a chance to reply, I turned and extended a hand to his friend, introducing myself. "Sonora said you're with the Tenth Cavalry. A mite far from home, aren't you?" I asked.

"The Army's cut down a lot in the last couple of years. Only about fifty-seven thousand in the whole shebang now, so they's usin' colonels for inspection duty. We're here as aides, and as an honor guard unit for Colonel Benjamin Grierson."

"How'd you get so lucky?" asked Sonora, looking over at the tents unhappily.

"Supposed to be a special detail," grunted the sergeant. "Ain't very excitin' but Ah wanted this postin' 'cause it pays extra. Ah even had to compete with some other sergeants for the job."

"How so?" I asked.

"Army had a contest, and as part o' the competition they held a surprise inspection. Checked everything from soup to nuts. Boiled it down to just two o' us. When they had us turn out for the full dress uniform inspection, it was so close they couldn't choose between us, so the colonel finally had us strip down. Sergeant James was always crisp as a new bill, but, as it turned out, he was wearin' store-bought civilian long johns. Most o' the men do 'cause they's more comfortable, but that was enough to disqualify him. Ah might've been wearin' them, too, but Ah'd heard about that little ol' trick from a captain Ah'd once served with. When the colonel saw Ah was the only one wearin' Army issue undergarments, Ah got the job."

"To the victor go the spoils," I joked.

"They treatin' you OK, Sarge?" Sonora was genuinely concerned.

"Sure, son. Ben Grierson's a good man. In fact, Ah once heard him take on another colonel from the Third Infantry who claimed we was nothin' more than a nigger unit. Said that he didn't want us forming up next to his men on parade drill. A real uppity sort. Well, Ah'll tell ya, Colonel Grierson laid into that son-of-a-bitch like Ah never seen done. Told him the Tenth was takin enemy positions while his men were still wipin' their asses in the latrines."

"Your unit has been getting some good press lately," I commented.

"Shit, a black man does his job well and all o' a sudden the press is surprised. Hell, there's been a whole bunch of black Army units, the Twenty-Fourth and Twenty-Fifth Infantry, for example, and the Ninth Cavalry. There've been black men fightin' all the way back to Bunker Hill. But you wanna know how it really is? The Tenth Cav' whups a few tired and hungry Injuns and all of a sudden we're heroes."

"I doubt they were that simple to beat," I said.

"Nate here's a real hero," offered Sonora, whacking his friend on the back again. "Medal and all. Bunch of 'Paches had a whole column pinned down. Ol' Nate here strolled up by his lonesome, calm as Sunday goin' to meetin', and took out five of 'em. They promoted him all the way up to sergeant-major."

"Ya always did talk too much," replied the sergeant. "And what do ya mean 'ol' Nate'? Ah kin still whup yo' ass any day."

"I'll give you that, Sarge," Sonora conceded in good humor.

"Right about one thing, though. Ya cain't git any better than this 'cause there ain't no black officers in this man's Army."

There was obviously a lot of depth, courage,

and humility to this grizzled old man, and I could sympathize with his disappointment.

"Give it time, Sarge," I said encouragingly, but there was no reply.

After an uncomfortable silence Sergeant Freeman turned to Sonora. "You boys had anything to eat?" When we shook our heads, he led us back to the mess tent and saw to it that we were fed.

Chapter Eighteen

Sergeant-Major Freeman, we soon learned, shared a two-man tent with Corporal Carl Mathews who we found arranging his haversack as we entered the tent. The contents of the pack scattered on the floor were fairly standard: a metal plate and eating utensils, a dozen or so slightly moldy hardtack crackers, a change of socks, matches, a twist of tobacco, a bag of coffee beans, his razor, and a small sewing kit. The daily rations also included about six ounces of pork (occasionally maggot-ridden), a few dried apples, beans, and a potato.

"Corporal," the sergeant asked after introducing us, "you suppose we could find quarters for these two stragglers?" Nate Freeman took three cups from off a tack box near his cot and reached for the coffee pot.

"If we move Johnson over in with Williams, they can use the extra tent. I'll go see to it, Sarge."

"Thanks, Carl."

Corporal Mathews finished folding his pack and left, dropping the tent flap down after him.

"Hope you boys take it black. Ain't got no cream or sugar, Isiquiel," Nate said with a shrug.

Sonora shot him a dirty look. "That's just fine."

"Fine with me, too," I said, chuckling.

"Sarge, you know anything about a herd of Spanish horses passing through here lately. They'd have a brand that looks something like this." I drew an EH in the dirt floor, closing it off as Pete Evans had described to make four boxes. I briefly explained my situation.

"Sorry, son. We only pulled in here two weeks ago and the colonel's had us camped back here the whole time. Only thing we've seen is the drill field, the back of the stable, and this tent city." He paused a moment in thought. "You boys might check with Major Gilbert, though. He's the fort's commanding officer. Ain't nothing goes on around here he don't know about. Tell ya what, Ah'll take ya over to see him soon as we get y'all settled."

"Don't know about Isiquiel, here," I said, tipping my coffee cup to an annoyed Sonora Mason, "but I won't be staying long. Say, any chance we can clean up before seeing the major?" I asked hopefully.

Sergeant Freeman shook his head. "You kiddin'? Around here? Hell, Ah've been ten years in the Southwest division, and been stationed in over a half dozen forts. Ain't seen a bathhouse yet. After a while ya just sort of forget your sense o' smell. Unless o' course you're an officer, that is."

"The bunks are ready, Sarge," Carl Mathews said, sticking his head through the tent flap.

I looked over at Sonora. "If I have to bunk with him, I sure hope it doesn't take too long to lose." I winked over at the sergeant.

"Lose? Lose what?" asked Nate.

"My sense of smell." Nate laughed and Sonora threw his empty coffee cup at my head as I quickly ducked out of the way.

Sergeant Freeman later accompanied us to the office of the fort's commander where we found Major Jeffery Gilbert seated behind an old, chipped flat-top desk. The rest of the office was equally Spartan, with only one other chair, which was currently occupied by Colonel Grierson. There was a flagpole in each corner, one for the flag, and the other for the unit's colors. A picture of President Lincoln hung on the wall behind the colonel, still draped, I noticed, with black ribbon.

Sergeant Freeman was the first to speak. "Beggin' the colonel's permission, sir. These men would like to ask the major a few questions. Ah can vouch for them if necessary, sir."

"Thank you, Sergeant-Major, that won't be necessary. What can we do for you gentlemen?"

There was a subtle but noticeable hesitation before the word "gentlemen", due I'm sure to our raggedy appearance.

"Colonel, I'm trailing after a herd of stolen horses that I believe passed through here, and thought the major or his men might have some information that could help me. The horses might have been wearing a Four box or an EH brand."

Major Gilbert nodded his head. "Yes, I remember the outfit. The herd didn't actually pass through the fort, mind you, one of my patrols came across it a few miles north of here." The major turned to the colonel. "Lieutenant Peters was leading at the time and brought their ramrod back here to the fort. Peters said the horses looked remarkably prime."

"I know the lad," commented the colonel. "He's a good judge of horseflesh."

"That sounds like them," I said, encouraged.

"I'm empowered to do the purchasing for the Army in this whole area, but, try as I might, I couldn't convince them to sell," the major added. "That ramrod was a real hardcase. Said we couldn't come close to the price he'd get elsewhere." Major Gilbert turned back to the colonel. "We could have really used those horses. I even tried to, shall we say, convince him to sell. Let on he was risking confiscation of the herd for Army use, but he knew the law and basically called my bluff."

"Sounds like whatever he knew of the law came from being on the wrong side of it, I'd say," Colonel Grierson commented. He had an annoying habit of continually drumming his fingers on the table top.

"What did this cowboy look like, Major?" I asked.

"Oh, about your height and build. Moustache, cleft chin. Wore a brace of Remingtons cross-draw style."

"Pierce," I said, nodding to Sonora. "Did he happen to mention where he was headed?'

"Not precisely, but, from the reports my patrols gave me, I'd say they were being driven north into California."

"That fits with what you figured," Mason commented, pushing his hat up. "Maybe the Army can help, eh?"

I looked back at the officers. "That herd was

stolen from a *Señor* Hernandez. I was scouting for him at the time, and have been trailing the herd ever since. Good men were killed and the future of two ranches depends on my catching those rustlers. And I might mention that one of the ranch owners is ex-regular Army. What do you say, could you spare some men to go after them with me?"

"That Pierce really rubbed me the wrong way," the major said, looking to the colonel for support.

"Then you'll help him?" asked Sonora.

"Wish we could," answered the colonel.

"Unfortunately there are several overlapping jurisdictions in this territory, such as the Department of the Interior and the militia. Hell, when Indians are involved, even the Society of Friends gets involved. In this case the robbery's a civil matter, and our federal troops have been prohibited from interfering in such things. You might try the territorial marshal," he suggested.

"Right now he's out in the field and, from what I hear, isn't expected back for a month," Major Gilbert informed us. "Maybe the Arizona Rangers could help?" he offered.

"No, they won't cross over into California, and I don't have time to wait for the marshal," I answered unhappily.

"Sorry, wish we could be of more help," the major said, shrugging his shoulders.

"Time to go, boys. These men got business, too." It was the sergeant speaking this time. "With your permission, sir," he added.

"You're dismissed, Sergeant," Colonel Grierson replied.

Nate Freeman held the door open for us, but, as

Sonora started for it, I paused and turned back toward the major.

"You have been a help, Major, and I appreciate it, but I got just one last question. Have any of your patrols reported a large group of Mexican *vaqueros* in the area?"

"*Vaqueros?* No, they haven't. Why? They part of the outfit that was hit?"

"That's right." I nodded.

"Friends of yours?" asked the colonel.

"I sure hope so," I answered as the sergeant closed the door behind me.

Chapter Nineteen

Sonora and I parted company the next morning. I didn't really expect him to get involved in my fight, but I did ask if he was going to stick around the fort.

"Any chance of you having a friendly chat with Chavez and his boys when they show up? You know, to help explain things."

He shook his head. "Wouldn't mind doing it for you, you know that, but I probably won't be here long enough to get the chance. Gonna be leavin' in a day or so. After all, I don't want to wear out my welcome. Besides, I'm supposed to hook up with some friends o' mine just south o' here. Sorry, but it's not likely we'll cross trails with them *vaqueros*."

That ended that. While it was possible the *vaqueros* might enter the fort and ask the right people about me, it was equally possible they'd just stock up quickly at the sutler's store and ride out so as not to waste any time. Furthermore, even if they did talk to Nate, or one of the other officers, they probably wouldn't trust the word of another *gringo*. I knew if that were the case and nothing else happened to change their mind, I'd still be in for it.

Sonora wished me luck as I rode out. I had been convinced ever since arriving at the fort that I knew where the herd was headed. *Don* Enrique had intended to drive his horses to California because the price was especially high there. Rosa, also, had described in detail her uncle's ranch in California, and how someone was trying to force him off his land.

Ordinary outlaws would have sold the horses the first chance they got. This bunch, however, had passed several towns and had turned down a generous and seemingly opportune offer by Major Gilbert. When combined with what Pete Evans had told me, things all began to make sense.

The whole scheme had been too elaborate for common bandits. It had been too well planned and funded from the start. The rustlers had followed us from the start without being detected. The raid had been carried out with military precision, and the thieves could apparently afford to risk holding out for a higher sale price. If Davies was powerful enough to try large-scale land grabbing, he could also fund a scheme such as this one. That's why I now rode as fast as I could straight toward our original destination, San Gabriel, right for Rosa's uncle's ranch in California.

Fortunately the vet had been right about those shoes, and the roan was acting as spry as ever. I was fairly certain the herd wouldn't be driven directly to Davies's own ranch; he would be too careful to allow that. But they wouldn't be very far away. I felt my best chance to find the herd would be to head directly to town and stake out Davies's outfit from there. Sooner or later someone would lead me to the horses, and, in the event the herd had already been broken up or sold intact, I'd at least be close to the culprits and their money.

Once into California the temperature cooled off some, as the hot dry sands began gradually changing to black soil, green grass, and rolling wooded hills. Game was more plentiful, too, and I was able to supplement the meager supplies I'd carried from the fort with an occasional rabbit, squirrel, or deer.

The roan responded well to the colder weather, and we started to make better time. That horse had served me well and I'd regret having to return him, but among other things I was still as determined as ever to recover my Morgan bay stallion.

I rode into San Gabriel around midday. Before leaving the roan at the livery, I asked the blacksmith, a big bearded Mormon named Jacob Browne, if he recognized the EH brand. He couldn't recall ever having seen it before, meaning the herd hadn't passed through town. I knew there hadn't been enough time to change the brands on that many horses, not at the pace they'd been moving.

Since Davies couldn't risk having stolen horses found on his property, he would have to corral the herd somewhere nearby. But where? The location would have to be close enough to his ranch to allow him to keep track of the herd, and to supply his men. There had to be an abandoned ranch, blind cañon, or enclosed pasture nearby, large enough to hide over 1,000 horses. To find it I would need a little more information. For a while I considered heading straight for the local saloon.

If anyone knows a town's goings-on, it's usually the barkeep and his local band of barflies, but by the same token it was likely some of the same men I was trailing would be there and they might get suspicious if too many questions were asked.

At this point I knew I was getting close and didn't want accidentally to tip my hand to any of the gang. Not only that, but I couldn't be sure whether or not Pierce would recognize me if we were to meet. I didn't know how close a look at me he'd taken while I was lying in that ravine. That's when the town's bank caught my eye. Reconsidering my options, and thinking it was as good a place as any to start, I opened the door and went in.

When you look like an old side of beef even the flies won't touch, it's hard to convince anyone to take you seriously. Whoever said—"It's difficult to believe what you say when your appearance speaks so loudly."—knew what he was talking about. Here I was in the San Gabriel Mortgage & Trust Bank, a total stranger, looking like something the cat dragged in and expecting the bank manager to answer delicate questions.

I'd learned enough about bluffing at poker to know that sometimes the more ludicrous something appears, or the more outrageous it seems, the quicker some folks are to believe it. Con artists often take advantage of the same principle.

Like the time Loco Larry Peters used a fake money-making machine as a bribe to get out of jail. It had lots of knobs and cranks on it, and turned out shiny new greenbacks every hour. The kicker was the chump who fell for it was the very same town sheriff who'd already arrested Loco for running still another scam.

That sheriff of all people should have known how crooked Peters was, but, strange as it may seem, he refused to believe a jailbird like Larry would ever be brazen enough to sell a lawman something so obviously fake. Since nobody could be that foolish, he rationalized, the machine must therefore be real. Curiously the idea of a machine falling into his hands that made real money was so ludicrous and Larry's pitch so smooth, the sheriff was forced to believe it. He bought Loco's sales pitch, hook, line, and sawbuck. Of course the marshal's greed was also a contributing factor, one the con artist was glad to take advantage of.

They never did catch Loco Larry, but eventually the sheriff ended up in his own jail after trying to spend those machine-made greenbacks. Seems the first couple of bills cranked out of the box, the ones the sheriff saw Larry Peters make, were real enough, but the rest, not surprisingly, turned out to be counterfeit.

As far-fetched as it seems, when suddenly forced to deal with something incredible, or something outrageous, many people, like the sheriff, simply can't handle it. Looking as misbegotten as I did, the last thing I would ever be mistaken for was a wealthy cattle baron, so that's exactly what I decided to play.

"Yes, sir," I said, sweeping the dust off my chaps with my hat as if I owned the place. "Just got into town and decided to cut right to the quick. As my old uncle Zeke always says, the best businessmen are the ones who get a jump on the competition."

The bank manager, Mr. Alfonse Norwell, a rather timid pencil pusher, was the epitome of the company man. With his pair of wire spectacles, thinning hair, shiny brown vest, and gold watch chain he might have stepped right out of one of those new dime novels.

The man was small-framed, he couldn't have stood more than five foot three and had absolutely no idea what I was talking about. Loud, boisterous speech apparently was not the norm in this rather sedate establishment, and he actually shuddered when I spoke. I was counting on that effect as well as the fact that I'd caught him off guard by brushing right past his secretary and straight up to his desk. I guess you could say I gave him the old bum's rush.

"Yep, sold my herd in Colorado for a pretty penny and came straight on here to Californy to buy land and stock it. Rode right through without a stop and that's a fact. Just got in . . . didn't even have a chance to change. Already got my eye on a nice little ranch right near here, next to the McFarlen place I think it is. Come to think of it, maybe I'll offer to buy him out, too." I wasn't giving Alfonse any time to stop and think. "Uncle Zeke always said not to fiddle-faddle around. Go right to the town banker, he'd say. They'll have all the low-down, if anyone will. So, now, Mister Norwell, you tell me how to go about buying this little parcel."

"Oh, I'm afraid that won't do," he said, gesturing to the chair in front of his desk. "But our bank does have some holdings in the next county you might be interested in. Can I have my secretary bring you some coffee?"

The act was working; he already smelled money to be had.

"Nope, don't think so. You know, once I got my mind set on something, I usually see it through,"

I bellowed. "And I already took a fancy to that ranch."

"Well, you see, sir, the property I believe you are talking about is already owned by a Mister Brett Davies."

"So tell me . . . what's his price? Everyone's got one," I said brashly, purposely brushing more dust off my shirt and onto his desk.

Norwell shook his head emphatically.

"What's the problem?" I asked.

"Well, to be perfectly frank, I believe you will be disappointed. Of course, I can't go into all the financial specifics, but I believe Mister Davies is currently trying to expand. In fact, I understand he is in the process of obtaining the McFarlen property next to his for himself. You see, he is a rather influential man around these parts and would be more interested in purchasing than selling."

For the right amount of money most bankers would sell their own mothers, yet it sounded to me like Mr. Norwell was more interested in furthering Mr. Brett Davies's goals than in listening to any counter offers.

"Well, you don't get to be influential without considering all your options, right, Mister Norwell?" I said, slapping him on the shoulder for added effect. "Now, if you'll just direct me to the Davies ranch, I believe it's the Four Box spread, right?" I asked.

"Yes, that is correct," he answered, adjusting his glasses. He seemed unusually agitated.

"Good, as I was saying, if you'll just point me in the right direction, I think I'll have a chat with this Mister Brett Davies. After I brush off some of this trail dust, that is. By the way, mind if I use your name by way of introduction?"

"Uh, certainly," he replied nervously. "Here let me draw you a map."

"Mister Norwell, I certainly am obliged." I shook his hand a little too firmly and turned to leave. "Oh, by the way," I added with a wink, "if I close this deal, there will be something in it for you, rest assured. But in case you meet up with this Mister Davies before I get a chance to talk to him, I'd appreciate it if you wouldn't mention our little conversation."

He nodded to me. "I think I understand."

I smiled back. "Right, no sense tipping my offer to him before I've had a chance to make it stick. Wouldn't be smart business, now would it?"

"No, of course not," he answered, wiping his forehead with a white silk handkerchief. "Rest assured confidentiality is a trademark of our establishment."

"Knew it would be, Mister Norwell, knew it would be," I said, slamming the door behind me.

From the map Mr. Norwell had drawn, I could see why Davies was so interested in the McFarlen place. Brett Davies had bought or stolen all the adjacent lands around until they formed a horseshoe, with the McFarlen ranch smack in its center.

The problem, however, was that the McFarlens had settled on and around the only principle source of water locally. Furthermore, his ranch was situated so as to be the first place travelers from the north and west would pass on the way to town. Someday San Gabriel would grow to attract business from Los Angeles or even from San Francisco, and it wasn't too difficult to imagine a railroad line being laid down. Should that ever happen, the McFarlens would be as wealthy as anyone could ever want. Unless, of course, Davies had his way.

I debated riding right out to the McFarlen Ranch to explain my situation and to enlist their help, but it occurred to me that *Don* Enrique might already have wired his brother-in-law about what had happened. If that were the case, McFarlen would probably blame me, too. I could be walking right into a noose.

Wired his brother. . . . That thought set me to reconsidering something else Pete Evans had said. When I had grilled Evans back in the Arizona Territory, he mentioned that Davies had gotten his information by wire. Logically the telegraph office would be the next place to check out.

For Davies to have known ahead of time a drive was even being planned, he would have to have read McFarlen's wires from *Don* Enrique. Since telegraphs are supposed to be confidential, and if that were, in fact, how the rustlers learned our plan, then either someone in the Hernandez camp was sending other telegraphs directly to Davies in California, or he was somehow having private messages intercepted. The latter made more sense to me. More importantly, if true, it also made the local operator suspect.

Even though Pete Evans had made it clear that Davies was in cahoots with someone in San Rafael, it was unlikely any of *Don* Enrique's *vaqueros* would know Brett Davies, a *gringo* from California. However, if Davies was clever or powerful enough to have telegraph messages intercepted, he easily could have sent someone ahead to San Rafael either to recruit a spy or personally to wire him back. Someone like this Luke Pierce, who apparently had led the rustlers who trailed us from the start.

That's why I headed over to the telegraph office next. Judging by appearances, my suspicions probably weren't too far off. The key-pad operator was a rather scrawny fellow with a nose like a ferret. He sported long, wide sideburns and had a nervous habit of constantly tugging his left earlobe. His vest was worn to a shine, and he favored a string tie worn over a stiff-collared white shirt. In general, he seemed a very uncomfortable sort.

I took out some cigarette paper and walked slowly up to his window where a sign read Luis B. Jacobs, Station Attendant. Acting once more as if I owned the place, I rolled a cigarette and struck a match on the sill. "Howdy," I said. "You Jacobs?"

"That's right," he answered. "What can I do for you?"

"Davies sent me."

"That so? Don't believe I know you," he said, glancing up at the mention of Davies's name. I leaned over the sill and blew some smoke into the room.

"No reason you should," I agreed, tossing away the match. "I'm new here."

"So what do you want?" he asked abruptly.

"Look, bub, I'm just following orders. Davies said to check with you and see if you've got anything new for him."

"He ain't paid me for that last bit," Jacobs replied angrily. "This ain't as simple as it seems, you know. I take a lot of risks."

That cinched it. I was on the right track.

"Look, all I know is what I was told to do. You got a problem, take it up with Pierce," I said. I was just playing along, sort of shooting for effect, but I'd definitely struck a nerve. His whole expression changed as he slumped back in his chair. Pierce must really be a hard one to contend with, I thought grimly.

"All right, all right. Tell Mister Davies nothing's come through here or gone out since that last message I gave him . . . the one from McFarlen." Jacobs started sweating and tugged nervously at his ear.

"Nothing from those *mejicanos?*" I asked.

"Nah. She ain't sent nothin' for some time."

That "she" caught me by surprise.

"She ain't, huh? Say, by the way, now that you mentioned it, I've always wondered how you fellers figure out if it's a guy or a gal talking, what with all that clicking?" I offered him some tobacco, which he refused.

"You mean if they don't mention it outright?" he asked.

I just nodded.

"Well, since there ain't many women operators around, after a while you can tell by the sender's touch. Now, on the other hand, if a man's sending a message for a woman you can sometimes pick up on the kind of phraseology women use. 'Course, that only comes with my kind of experience." He was calming down some, regaining his composure. "Just between you and me," he added, "I ought to get more respect for what I do."

"Couldn't agree with you more." I nodded.

"Always thought this job was pretty complicated myself."

"Darn' tootin' it is," he said boastfully.

"And I'll bet an expert like you could even tell if a message came from a wife talking to a husband, or say a girl talking to her uncle?"

"Sure as hell could. For example, I know those last few messages to Davies came from a woman, and that she was usin' the same dispatch office as the earlier ones sent by that chili-dippin' brother-in-law of McFarlen's down south."

Now I was really puzzled. Who could it be?

"Thought I heard Pierce mention something about a daughter or niece, or something," I said.

"Not so's I know," he said, scratching his head. "But it could have been, though. See, I picked up what went on between the Mex and his grease-lovin' brother-in-law, McFarlen. The messages from the girl to Davies came later, but they didn't have no name on them."

"So how'd you know they came from the same place."

"Easy. Same operator. Kinda like readin' a signature."

I'd been lucky enough so far, and didn't want to spoil things, so I decided to cut it short.

"Mister Davies told me to tell you to sit tight and keep quiet. But, look, don't talk to no one unless I tell you, and, in the meantime, I'll see what I can do about your pay. But don't expect too much," I added. "Like I said, I'm new here."

"All right, I'll see ya later," he replied. Jacobs turned back to the keys as another message came in and I left with more questions than before.

Chapter Twenty

For the next three days I camped out in the hills north of the 4 Box Ranch, watching the goings-on from hiding. Whenever riders left the ranch, I'd follow, but inevitably they'd simply ride the fence line, or head back into town for supplies. On two separate occasions I spotted Luke Pierce riding my Morgan and had to restrain myself from repaying his favors with a head shot.

Finally, on the fourth day, a couple of riders left early, seemingly going about their usual rounds. After about fifteen minutes, however, one of the men split away, taking a different trail from any previously used, north up into the hills.

I followed him for two and a half hours until coming to the front of a high rock face where he'd suddenly and completely disappeared. I rode up and down the path, searching, for about twenty minutes until finally returning to the spot where I'd lost him. I sat there studying the wall, trying to spot the entrance to what had to be a hidden cañon. There were a few gaps in the wall that all ended in solid rock and several tree trunks that seemed too large to move.

I cursed my luck and was just about to call it quits when I spotted a hawk diving down on a sparrow. Both flew at top speed straight through the trees, yet neither came back out. Not one to distrust Mother Nature, I refused to believe they'd both flown blindly into a solid wall, and a closer inspection confirmed my suspicions.

It was a beautiful job of disguise, one so clever even old Ali Baba and his Arabs would have been proud of it. Two large clumps of trees grew in opposite curves forming an arch. The middle three trees had been hollowed out, dug up, and replaced in the same spot. From a distance the thick green cover growing down from the end trees hid the fact that the whole middle section of trees was dead.

There was a large rope and pulley affair tied to some clusters of rock located on both sides of the wall. When tripped from a lever hidden in a notch in the wall, the balance was sprung and the rocks dropped, pulling the middle section of tree trunks up, roots and all. It was like one of those castle drawbridges Ma had described when she read to me about Arthur and Lancelot.

Behind the door was a long passage leading out into a blind cañon. There I found green pasture, a line shack at the far end, and a herd of Spanish EH brand horses grazing contentedly.

So far nobody had spotted me. The smart thing to do now would be to hightail it straight back to the McFarlen Ranch, and then over to the sheriff's. That would have been the smart thing, but instead I decided to snoop around the line shack.

I suppose I knew, deep down, that simply recovering the herd for ***Don*** Enrique and his relatives, the McFarlens, was the important thing, and that it would be sufficient to clear my name, but I had a more personal score to settle. I wanted to be able to prove conclusively that Davies and Pierce were behind the rustling. Men had died and many other lives placed at risk because of the greed of these two men. I wasn't about to let them get away with it.

Sneaking around the side of the shack, I listened for a while to the three men inside. I was on foot holding my hand over the roan's mouth to quiet him down while I eavesdropped. It never occurred to me that anyone would bother to build a back door to such a small cabin.

"Hold it right there, mister." The voice was deep but not nearly as commanding as the *click* from the hammer being pulled back on the revolver. "What are you doing here?"

"Relax," I replied. "I'm looking for Curly, Curly Edwards." I turned around slowly. It was a quick gamble. His was the only name I'd overheard them use and I had to say something. "You can put it away," I said, gesturing toward his gun. "Luke Pierce sent me to help out."

"We'll see about that. Now move." As we rounded the front, the other two cowboys came out the door. "What's up Jeff? Who's this?"

I recognized Curly's voice. As expected, he was bald as an egg.

"That's what I'd like to know. Says Pierce sent him. You know him?"

"Never saw him before. How about you, Andy?" He was addressing the cowboy I'd followed into the valley.

"Nope. And Pierce never said nothin' to me about expecting anyone to show up, neither."

"Of course not," I answered. "I just hitched up. Been on the run and had to stay low. Came out here 'cause I used to ride with Luke a few years ago back, in West Texas."

They looked at each other, unsure of how to proceed. Constant reference to Pierce's name had created some doubt in their minds, so I quickly answered their questions with enough assurance to make my story convincing.

"Think about it. How else would I have been able to find my way in here?" I asked. "And look here," I said, pointing to the brand on the roan. "Pierce himself picked this one out for me. Haven't even had time to switch him over to the Four Box yet."

That seemed to cinch things for them, at least for the time being. They holstered their guns and the one named Andy went back into the cabin.

"Just one question. What were you doin' sneakin' 'round the side of the shack?" Jeff asked. He apparently was the cautious type.

"Like I said, I'm on the run. I don't know you boys, so I thought I'd better check things out before knocking on a strange door. Wouldn't you?"

"Guess so. All right, come on in. Want some coffee?" he asked, seemingly convinced.

"Don't mind if I do."

After a couple of hours of small talk I got enough details out of them to learn Davies was finally planning his big raid. In spite of the loss of the herd, the McFarlens still hadn't been convinced to sell, and Davies had run out of patience. When a person has both money and the power it brings, there comes a time when he begins to feel almost god-like. Or at least so I've been told. Davies apparently no longer worried about appearances or consequences. I learned the attack was planned for sometime soon, but none of the three cowpokes knew exactly when.

My chance to break loose came when Curly and Andy got up to do a once around look-see.

"That reminds me, Curly," I said. "Luke wanted me to ride with you. Said you could show me the layout.

They all seemed easily impressed that I was on a first name basis with Pierce.

"That's why I asked for you first, remember?"

"That's right, he did," Jeff added helpfully.

"OK with me," Andy added. "I've had more than enough saddle time lately."

"Great, let's go," I said, quickly figuring that one on one odds outside were better than three to one inside.

We mounted up but managed to ride only about 200 yards before we closed with a large group of armed riders.

Even if he weren't riding my Morgan bay stallion, I'd still have recognized Luke Pierce. My height, my color hair, and twin Remington .44s worn cross-draw style, pistol butts forward. He had my Henry in the saddle scabbard, but was also carrying a Sharps rifle in his right hand.

Pa's advice to me as a boy after I'd busted knuckles with Billy Watson suddenly came back to me. "You may not like it, but remember, Son, iffen you are forced to fight, hit first and hit hard." The problem now was how to do that against so many.

We cantered straight up to the group, stopping directly in front of Pierce.

"Howdy, Luke," I said calmly.

He stared back at me, and then over to Curly, puzzled.

"Who the hell is this, Pierce?" asked a big red-headed man riding just off to his left. He was about six feet and wore a brown hunting jacket over a vest. There was no waist gun visible, but, when he turned to the side, I noticed twin shoulder holsters.

"I don't know, Mister Davies," Pierce replied. "Never saw him before."

"Luke, you might not recognize me, even though you are riding my horse, but I'm sure you'll remember a friend of mine," I said, looking the group over.

"Yeah, and who might that be?" he asked.

"A little Indian boy who's now lying in a grave near a town called Buffalo Grove. One who's only crime was trying to keep some cowardly back-stabbin' thieves from taking his horse." I looked over at Davies. "You see, Brett, aside from bush-whacking honest men for you, Luke here gets a kick out of holding children from behind while his old friend Reynolds stabs them dead. 'Course, now that we finally met up, Reynolds won't be doing that any more."

"You know you're gonna die for that," muttered Pierce angrily.

"Well, Luke, you tried once and failed," I said calmly. "Funny how things have a way of catching up on a feller. You're gonna die, Luke, just like your friend Reynolds did. I'm going to see to it. And that goes for you, too, Davies."

"There won't be a next time," Davies replied angrily. "Take care of him, Pierce."

Luke dropped his reins and he swung the Sharps rifle upward. He apparently had grown to trust that Morgan, who was usually a pretty calm riding horse. Usually, that is, but not always. Sprout had spent over a month helping me teach that stallion a variety of Kiowa tricks, and the kid was about to get his revenge.

At the sound of my whistle that Morgan started bucking like a Missouri mule sitting on a beehive. The heavy weight of Pierce's rifle helped throw him backward off the bay, and every horse nearby was either kicked or spooked into a frenzy.

Three riders immediately toppled over sideways, and, as I galloped past, Davies was knocked from his saddle by my outstretched forearm. The chocolate roan reacted to my spurs in a flick, darting forward through the gap created by the stallion's antics. We raced away with the Morgan in full pursuit, responding to my whistles.

I rode out through the pass, hesitating only long enough to spring the pulleys. As soon as we broke out of the trees, I jumped horses. The *vaqueros* call it the leap of death, and Kiowas learn it as children. At a full gallop the rider comes out of his stirrups and jumps over to a second horse running alongside. It has to be timed just right or the rider can easily break his neck.

The roan had been a good steady mount and, much to his credit, stayed right up with us the whole way, but I wanted to be riding that Morgan stallion. I knew what he was capable of in a pinch, and with that gang on my tail I was going to need all the lead time I could get. I knew there was no way Davies would hold back now. He would go after the McFarlens and take what he wanted, and there was no one around strong enough to stop him.

I had to reach the ranch in time to warn them. McFarlen needed to prepare for the attack, and I was determined to let him know where the herd was hidden, or die trying.

I was between the horns and the wall. Brett Davies and his bunch were after me, and somewhere ahead was a group of ***vaqueros*** coming my way, just itching to lynch me. Even so, I was now so mad none of it mattered to me. I'd made a promise to Rosa Hernandez and I aimed to keep it.

Chapter Twenty-one

We came galloping through the trees, the stallion snorting like a demon possessed, the roan following right on his tail.

After racing through the gates of the McFarlen place, I fired a warning shot. It was a risky thing to do with nervous ranch hands around to fire back, but I hoped I was moving too fast for anyone to take clean aim.

I hauled rein and the Morgan slid about twenty feet, not stopping until his front hoofs were practically on the front doorstep. As I leaped from the saddle, several of the wranglers came running up from behind with their guns drawn.

I faced a large, bearded man standing on his front porch, cradling a sawed-off double-barreled twelve gauge in his arm.

"McFarlen?" I coughed. He nodded back at me. "There's not much time to explain. Brett Davies and about fifty of his riders are right behind me and they're aiming to burn you out. They're the same ones who rustled your brother-in-law's herd. Trust me, I was the scout for *Don* Enrique."

McFarlen's wife appeared in the doorway. She was a small, heavy-set, but attractive lady who I guessed to be in her late forties.

"Ana, git in the house and open the rifle case!"

She disappeared inside as McFarlen turned around. He was about to gesture to one of his men, but the cowboy, already thinking ahead, had begun to slam closed the heavy shutters running the length of the house.

Being ex-military, McFarlen had built the ranch house as best he could in order to protect it from attack. Even so, with only eleven men, I knew it would be hard to hold it against a sudden massed assault.

Some of the men were already running through the door and taking positions at window slots that were cut into the shutters. A short stocky Oriental in a leather apron began desperately banging on a dinner chime. He was trying to attract the attention of the other wranglers still out in the far corral, to get them headed back to the big house.

"With that many coming at us, we'll need to send someone for help," McFarlen said, looking around desperately.

At precisely that moment a big bore rifle, probably a Sharps, rang out and one of McFarlen's wranglers was flung forward to the ground, dead before his face ever smacked dirt. Any chance of getting outside help died with him. Other shots ricocheted on both sides of us.

Yanking the Henry from my saddle scabbard, I gave the bay a whack on the rump and wheeled toward the door, barely clearing it as three or four bullets splintered the jamb near my face. After slamming the door shut with my back, I slumped down and took stock of the situation around me.

Counting Mrs. McFarlen who held a Remington rifle in her arms like she knew how to use it, we made a total of thirteen. Some of the men were grabbing rifles out of a long wall rack and handing out boxes of ammunition. The rest had already started shooting back.

McFarlen positioned himself next to the far window. He had laid the shotgun by his side and was shouldering a long Springfield .45–70 Trapdoor rifle. The cabin walls were solid log and seemed strong enough, but we were taking a tremendous barrage of rifle fire. At this rate, it was only a matter of time before the windows and doors would splinter.

Eventually, I feared, Davies would either try to rush us in force or burn us out. I prayed the McFarlens' outer storeroom had none of the blasting powder usually found on most ranches.

"Is there a cellar exit to the back, or an escape tunnel around here?" I asked hopefully.

McFarlen shook his head. "Never had the chance to finish one. Ever since we got here, I've been fighting just to finish the basic framework and to get the corrals put up." His eyes never left the Springfield's sights the whole time he spoke.

I managed to pick a rider off with my Henry, but there were plenty more to go around. I thought about our chances. It was hot and the only water available was from an outside well. Even though the house was inaccessible from two sides, we were outnumbered and boxed in.

"I'm open to suggestions!" McFarlen called out, similarly aware of the hopelessness of our predicament.

"Well, we could move back East and take up dairy farming," I quipped. "I for one would be glad to go with you. You suppose they'll let us leave here peacefully?"

Just then a large slug burst one of the shutters and took out the windpipe of a cowboy at the far end of the room.

"I doubt it." McFalen shrugged, chambering another shell. He gestured toward his wife. "I wouldn't mind this so much but for my Ana. She's been as fine a wife as any man could hope for, and don't deserve this." His sadness, evident as he paused to watch her, was understandable.

She had long black hair worn in a bun on top. It was beginning to gray, but I thought it gave her face more character. Her bluish-gray calico dress was worn but clean, and she had on a full-length apron. Around her neck was an oversize silver crucifix, giving her the appearance of someone who was used to the finer things in life but who was now making do with less.

What I could see of the main room confirmed my suspicion that she kept both herself and her husband's home as proper as their means allowed. I doubted that she was the type ever to complain, and was sure that, if need be, she would gladly give her life to save her husband. McFarlen was right, she didn't deserve this.

Their home was pretty well shot up by now and most of us were holding low, unable to take careful aim without exposing ourselves. I made up my mind that I was not going to die on my knees, trapped inside this house.

"Maybe we could take this fight out to them and buy you enough time to slip her out of here," I suggested.

"You might be able to hide out somewhere in back."

I looked over as Mrs. McFarlen's rifle bucked in

her arms. "It's not right for her to go out like this, but, judging by what I see, she won't leave here without you."

McFarlen nodded to me, tears welling in his eyes. The room was in ruins and several of the men were already wounded.

"Boys, what say we go out on our feet, fighting? At least we can try to give the McFarlens a chance!" I shouted at the others.

"I'm with ya, mister," one of them replied. "Anything's better than this."

A few other cowboys nodded. They all fired a round or two, and then bunched up behind me at the door.

"When we spring this door, you two cover the missus," I said, pointing to the pair on my left. "Try to block Davies's line of fire and let the McFarlens slip out around back. The rest of you head with me to the corral. If we can get into the horses, maybe we can scatter things up and use 'em for cover." I tried to sound more optimistic than I really felt.

We let go another volley as McFarlen pulled the bolt on the door. Seven of us poured out the door, firing as we went. I had my Henry in my hand and the Navy Colt fully loaded in my holster. I levered another round and fired the rifle.

We made it through the door and onto the verandah, but not much farther.

Davies and his men had left the cover of the trees. They had chosen that very moment to remount and were now charging down on us. One man dropped on my right, shot in the leg. We were firing as fast as we could, but they kept on coming. There was no place for us to go, so we spread out in the open all along the verandah.

I was so mad I didn't care about dying just as long as we took some of the 4 Boxers with us. I didn't expect I'd have to wait very long for my time to come when, all of a sudden, I heard a loud Comanche yell in the distance off to our left.

Riding down off the ridge and heading for us at full tilt was a solid line of *vaqueros*, standing in the stirrups and firing as they rode. I never saw a more glorious sight, and several of the ranch hands shouted their relief.

I fired my rifle at the nearest 4 Box rider, sending him off his horse and into a corral log. The arrival of all those *vaqueros* at the same time as the 4 Box attack was purely coincidental, but it sure caught them off guard.

Davies didn't know where to turn first. Instead of finishing off a few lone ranch hands, his men now found themselves trapped between a solid row of rifles on one side, and twenty charging *vaqueros* barreling down on them from another.

Several cowboys were immediately shot off their horses and an instant later it became one big free-for-all. Once everyone collided, the *vaqueros* began using their machetes. Up close, it wasn't a pretty sight.

I fired my Henry point-blank into a rider coming straight at me. He took it right in the chest, toppling off backward in a sort of slow roll.

Off to my left I noticed Chango Lopez on foot, pursuing a Davies man who, to my horror, turned suddenly and shot him point-blank in the side. For an instant I could see the look of terror on the cowboy's face as Chango, seemingly unaffected, grabbed him up in those big arms of his and crushed his skull.

At this point everything was up for grabs.

I emptied my rifle and dropped it on the porch. Charging into the fracas, I tried to find Luke Pierce. I turned straight into a second group of horsemen charging down at us. Davies must have held Pierce and thirty or so others in reserve, and they'd waited until now to attack. The element of surprise created by the *vaqueros'* arrival was about to be eliminated, overcome by the sheer force of numbers.

With almost military precision Pierce galloped his men in a straight column along the edge of the long barn, about 100 yards from the main fight, and then wheeled left to face us. A company of Rangers couldn't have executed the maneuver any better.

"Damn," I grunted. "Look out, boys, they're charging!" I shouted to those around me.

"*¡Atrás, muchachos!*" a *vaquero* called out.

Pierce and his men spurred their horses, and almost as one they leaped forward at us. I was on foot, surrounded by horses and falling bodies. Even if we had had more men, there wasn't time to bring enough guns together to stop the charge. I swear I caught Luke Pierce staring at me with an evil grin on his face. It must have been obvious to him that he had us dead to rights.

The 4 Box line was galloping straight at us about twenty-five yards away when I noticed a movement on the roof of the long barn, right behind Pierce's men. Fifteen men suddenly stood up and simultaneously fired one tremendous volley. The blast was so loud I flinched, but surprisingly the fire was directed downward, right into the back of that charging line of men and horses.

Instantly about half of the men were shot out of their saddles, and several horses flipped horribly, end over end.

I looked back up to see a line of Mexicans on the roof, whistling and jeering as they continued their withering fire. Sonora Mason stood in the middle of them, laughing.

"I'll be damned," I muttered, waving up to him.

Luke Pierce miraculously survived the volley, managing to turn his horse at a dead run and flee the scene. I caught a glimpse of Brett Davies trying to escape, but I ran around him and blocked his path. Davies pulled up short once he recognized me.

"You son-of-a-bitch!" he shouted, spurring his horse in an attempt to run me over. Davies came on so fast I was forced to fan my pistol from the draw, slip shooting from the hip. The first bullet took him in the right eye and, as he raised his hands up in reflex, the second and third slammed into his chest. His horse was jerked back by the pull on the reins and fell over on him, crushing an already dead body.

I looked around, realizing that the tide now had turned in our favor. Several of the cowboys and a few *vaqueros* were dead, but even though both groups were still mixed together in fierce fighting, it was clear the 4 Box brand was losing.

Over to my left a cowboy was about to use his rifle to club McFarlen from behind. I pulled my Bowie from my boot sheath and threw it right to the hilt into his back. Davies's men evidently intended to go down fighting.

Wheeling to my right, I found Chavez alone, fighting off three cowboys. He was mounted on a large gray with a long dark mane and tail, but the 4 Box riders had his horse trapped between them. One was blocking the front while the other pressed his horse in from behind. A third cowboy was keeping Chavez busy on his right. They were too far away for me to reach in time, especially on foot. Since I had emptied my Colt and was now without knife or rifle, all I could do was wait for the inevitable outcome. I stood there watching the fight as a helpless observer.

It was obvious the *caporal* was doomed. There was no way he could react in time to protect himself from a three-sided attack. At least none that I could think of.

Just then Chavez drew his machete out from its sheath, and with a loud yell struck out violently to his right, embedding the blade into the nearest cowboy's neck. As the remaining riders in front and behind were preparing to shoot, his horse did something I'd never seen before, or since for that matter.

That gray rose up on its haunches, sort of like a dog begging, and launched itself straight up in the air. Chavez actually seemed to be part of his mount. I have seen Comanches do some incredible things on horseback, but nothing like this.

The front hoofs knocked the cowboy right off his horse, which then spooked and immediately hightailed it out of there with its rider angling behind, hung up in his stirrup. And as if that weren't enough, the gray, which was now up in the air and horizontal, kicked straight out backward like a mule.

Six feet off the ground with a rider sitting calmly aboard, and this horse is kicking out backward like a mule! The cowboy attacking from behind was caught completely by surprise. Hit full force in the chest by both rear hoofs, he was flung from his chestnut like a rag doll. I hate to think how many ribs were broken. Every 4 Box rider who saw that move knew it was all over, and those who were still able immediately hightailed it for the next territory, our bullets flying after them.

I stood there with my mouth hanging open as Chavez calmly rode up to me. I wasn't sure how he would react to my presence amidst all this bloodshed. My hand rested on the butt of my pistol. It was empty, but at least he didn't know that.

"That was a hell of a trick, *caporal,*" I said, testing the waters.

"*Cabriol,*" he replied. "I teach you sometime." He suddenly broke into a grin, and tipped his hat back as Francisco and Armando rode up to join us.

"I don't understand," I said, surprised at the change in attitude. "I was sure you'd think I was one of their gang. Figured you'd want to shoot me on sight. What made you change your mind?" I asked.

"*Sí,* it is true, we did," Francisco replied in English.

"But, then *Señorita* Rosa try to convince us otherwise. *Qué genio,* what a temper! When she got through yelling, even the *caporal* stopped to think."

"We were going to hang you," Armando added somewhat matter-of-factly. "But you are a hard man to catch."

"*Sí,* you were very clever. But the *caporal* began to wonder why you don't just disappear completely. You know, *compadre,* sometimes your tracks were a little too easy to follow. So, when we seen you coming out of *Señora* Ana's cabin, fighting with the others, we knew that the *Señorita* Rosa had been right all along," Francisco added.

I felt the tension drain from my body as my hand dropped back down to my side. We all returned to the cabin to check on the McFarlens and to tend to our wounded. I met up with Sonora Mason as he was climbing down from the barn.

"I thought you said you weren't headed this way," I said.

"Wasn't at first. But my *amigos* and I thought you might need some help with those rustlers. Besides, we never were ones to pass up a good fight. No sense lettin' you have all the fun," he replied. "And who knows, now that he's down a few men, *Don* Enrique might be in a mood to hire us."

"You? Work for a living?" I asked, surprised by the thought of it.

"Truth is things been a little dry lately. Ranch work doesn't seem as unattractive as it used to."

"Especially if you're working for an outfit like Hernandez, right?" I added.

Sonora just shrugged. "Care to put in a good word for us?"

Looking around, I smiled and shook my head. "Don't really think that's gonna be necessary. You did a good enough job of it yourself. Thanks, *hombre*."

Chapter Twenty-two

The Sharps is as accurate as it is powerful. That's why it's often referred to as "Old Reliable", and, in the hands of an expert shot like Luke Pierce, it can be downright devastating. Pierce had holed up in a rocky notch halfway up a steep cliff with an open view of the valley I'd chased him into. He had a clear line of fire and was simply biding his time until I came into range.

Unfortunately he seemed continually frustrated by the fact I had already backtracked several times, as if double checking the valley for something. Each time I turned away just before entering the range of his Sharps rifle. Luke Pierce was a careful man. He wasn't about to spoil his chance to kill me by rushing his shot.

For a solid week I had pursued him south until he finally decided to stop running and prepare an ambush. Pierce had no trouble recognizing me, even from his high perch, or so he thought. Fact is, at that distance, my hat and buckskin shirt made quite an improvement on Sonora Mason who was well mounted on my Morgan bay.

Mason knew the area much better than I did, and had been helping me track Pierce all week. By the end of the third day Sonora had already guessed the exact spot Pierce would choose to make his stand.

I was sitting on a ledge just above Luke Pierce, watching the whole show. I'd reached the summit above and behind his position a good two hours earlier, and had begun gradually working my way down. I rested a spell, watching from above while Pierce followed Sonora Mason back and forth in his sights.

The anger welled up in me as I watched what otherwise would have been my own ambush taking place. Sonora carefully criss-crossed the valley once more out of range, but this time Pierce set his rifle down and picked up his canteen, allowing himself to take a drink.

I wasn't about to wait for another chance, so I swung forward off the ledge, dropped down, and landed right in front of Pierce. He reacted quickly, springing to his feet and at the same time flinging himself backward out of the way of my punch.

I hit him running, plowing into his gut with my right shoulder. Pierce went down hard, but, as I grabbed for his neck, he kicked sideways catching me behind my left knee. His kick caught me off guard, forcing me to roll over twice before I could regain my balance.

I stood back up and turned to face him, but Luke was already heading for his rifle, which had fallen on the ground on the far side of a waist-high rock.

I flung myself toward him, but Pierce reached the rifle before I did and grabbed it up on the run. He took several more steps before finally stopping at the edge of the cliff, turning quickly toward me while at the same time cocking the Sharps.

I was at a dead run aiming straight for him. When suddenly faced with the muzzle end of a loaded rifle, I knew I could no longer stop in time to take cover. There was no choice but to continue running forward, as fast as I could. Just as Luke's finger tightened on the trigger, I flung myself down, diving forward with my arms stretched out. Pierce fired as I dived over the rock.

I had somersaulted down into a barrel roll scarcely in time, so close I could feel the rifle's muzzle blast a bullet the length of my back. Coming out of the roll, I jumped to my feet, took four or five steps forward, and launched myself, this time with both boots out in front. My flying kick caught Pierce squarely in the chest, knocking him backward off his feet.

I fell flat on my back, landing hard with my legs dangling over the edge of the cliff. Luke hit the ground a lot farther down. Gasping and panting I quickly dragged myself back a foot or two and went limp. It was several minutes before I finally stopped shaking, regained my wind, and was able to get up. I looked over the edge and saw Luke Pierce, or what remained of him, crumpled on the rocks below.

After returning to San Gabriel, Sonora and I rejoined the rest of the men at the McFarlen Ranch. Chavez had moved the herd back to town and an auction had already been announced. Fortunately, as it turned out, those horses brought the highest sale prices ever recorded in that part of the state.

The bank was to have a new manager, too.

Seems Mr. Norwell became convinced after a brief discussion with McFarlen that it would be better for his health to reside in some other climate. "Any other climate but this one," I believe was how McFarlen put it. Not surprisingly the bank became very supportive of Norwell's decision to resign, especially after learning the profits from the McFarlen sale wouldn't be deposited in their bank until after a new manager was appointed.

Chavez and the rest of his men were becoming increasingly anxious to return home, so the *caporal* decided to telegraph *Señor* Hernandez. *Don* Enrique was informed of our success, but unfortunately Chavez also had to include a list of the men we'd lost. I accompanied the *caporal* to the telegraph office and was pleased but somehow not surprised to find there was now also a new operator. Luis B. Jacobs had suddenly taken ill and decided to leave town, coincidentally disappearing about the same time as the bank manager, Mr. Norwell.

Rosa Maria telegraphed us back from San Rafael. Her father was recuperating well, but was not yet able to make the trip into town. However, he was delighted at the good news and gladly gave Chavez permission to return whenever the *caporal* felt the McFarlens could handle things on their own. Rosa also asked Chavez to give me her regards and mentioned both she and her father were anxious to thank me in person.

Given the Spanish constraints for proper behavior, simple regards was about all one could expect from the daughter of a *hacendado*, but I could read between the lines. She hadn't forgotten me, and, as far as I was concerned, that was more than enough.

As anxious as we all were to return to Mexico, we were equally sorry to have to part company with the McFarlens. Ana had become something of a second mother to many of the men, and a better cook we never met. Even as busy as Mr. McFarlen was rebuilding his ranch and organizing the sale of the herd, he always had time to help the men with their own individual problems, such as making sure Chango got the necessary medical attention to help him recover.

He personally vouched for us in town so there wouldn't be any problems refitting for the trip, and he let everyone know there was a standing job offer for any of the men who might someday decide to return.

The trip back to Mexico, thankfully, was uneventful. We made good time, arriving at the hillsides overlooking San Rafael early in August. Ricardo, who had stayed behind at the *hacienda* while his leg healed, came riding up to meet us. The men all cheered as one, knowing they were home at last.

"*¿Hola,* Ricardo . . . *que hay?*" shouted Chavez, greeting the young *vaquero*.

Ricardo looked over at me and then back at Chavez, groping for an explanation.

Señorita Rosa was right all along about him, Chavez explained, answering Ricardo's doubts about me.

"*Lo siento,* Ricky," I quickly added. "You left me no choice."

"*Yo tambien,*" he said, rubbing his leg. "My leg is better."

Chavez then asked about his boss.

"*Don* Enrique is much better now and is on his way here. He should join us soon," Ricardo answered in Spanish. He then rattled off something too quickly for me to follow.

"He mention whether or not anything's happening in town?" I asked Francisco.

"*No, mucho,*" he answered, shrugging his shoulders. "You know, that pueblo, she never really changes much." He winked at Armando, who was sitting off to my side on a buckskin mare named Canela, and added: "Except that *Señorita* Rosa is already there in San Rafael with some of our men."

Armando grinned and slapped me on the back. "I know at least one *vaquero* who will be glad to see her, eh?"

"That'll be enough, 'Mando," I said, feigning displeasure. I turned back to face Chavez.

"*Caporal,* it's been a long ride to get back to where we started from. You still have a problem with my seeing Rosa?"

"Perhaps we should finish that fight we had at the *hacienda,* eh, *gringo?*" Chavez answered slowly, staring ahead in thought. "You know . . . for the benefit of the men."

"*¿Tu crees?*" I groaned. "That really what you want?"

He turned in the saddle, adjusted his sombrero, and shook his head. "They say the hunter learns to respect his prey. Well, I have argued with you, and I have hunted after you. Even so, I end up fighting at your side. And now I ride with you. I know Rosita all her life and only want what is best for her. If she feels you are best for her, I will no longer disagree." He offered me his hand.

"Although only God knows what she sees in you," he added, laughing.

Relieved, I shook with him and replied: "You are a hard taskmaster, *caporal*, but any man would be proud to count you among his friends."

"So are you two going to spend all day long here grinning at each other, or are we going into town?" Francisco asked impatiently.

"Well, I don't know about you *vaqueros*, but the first thing I'm gonna do is take a bath and finally get a shave," I replied, rubbing my chin.

Chavez looked at me, and then back at the rest of the men. "*¡Yo no!*" He flicked his hand up to his mouth in the universal gesture for drink, and shouted: "*¡Vamos a la cantina, muchachos!*"

"*¡Adelante, caporal!*" they yelled almost in unison.

Before I knew what was happening, I was alone sitting on my horse in a swirl of dust. When it cleared, I found myself looking down on a bunch of wild *mejicanos* racing ahead at a dead run toward town. Or rather, I should say, straight for Las Tres Campanas. I shortened my reins some and cantered the bay leisurely after them.

Chapter Twenty-three

There was only one bathhouse in town, but I was determined at long last to take advantage of the opportunity and clean up some before anything else happened. As long as we smelled the same, none of the men paid much attention, but, after all the time we'd spent on the trail, no decent woman would want to be in the same room with us.

I for one decided not to meet Rosa Hernandez again until I'd washed the topsoil off and scrubbed my face clean. Trail-wise or not, someone of her upbringing would be used to the finer things in life, and, if I was to have any chance with her father, I'd have to start looking the part. Or at very least make sure I smelled better than a used saddle blanket.

The local bathhouse wasn't much when viewed from the outside. The inside wasn't any better, looking more like an old barn than anything else. Were it not for all the soapy water sloshed on the floor and a table full of half dried towels, the place might easily have been mistaken for an old abandoned shack.

There were four rooms that consisted primarily of large sheets hung from iron hooks that were bolted into the rafters. The owner was a heavy-set, elderly Irish-Mexican named Paco Fitzhugh. Although Paco supposedly ran the place, all he really ever did was sit in a rocking chair at the entrance and rake in the money. All of the physical work was done by two young boys, Pablo and Mario, who cleaned towels, mopped floors, poured water, lit the customer's cigars, and made runs across the street to fetch drinks from the *cantina*.

The tips they made might have provided the boys with a decent living, if only Fitzhugh had let them keep some. Unfortunately Paco Fitzhugh also owned the house where the boys' mother lived, and claimed their tips as part of her rent. The fact that their mother, a short fat woman named Consuela, also did his cooking and cleaning didn't seem to matter much to him, either.

Fitzhugh liked to take things easy, and owning the bathhouse was an easy way for him to make a living. All he needed was a place for customers to bathe, water, towels, and soap. At least that's the way he saw it. So he had the building built as quickly and cheaply as possible. Once it served his purpose, he wasted no more time on it.

The bathhouse was such a rough cut and dirty affair the first sight of it made folks south of the border wonder how he could attract clients, let alone turn a profit, even if it did provide the only indoor bath for over 800 square miles.

What made the Fitzhugh bathhouse profitable, aside from his criminal frugality, were the tubs. The Fitzhugh bathtubs were legendary in these parts. Those four tubs had come all the way from France, originally shipped through Vera Cruz and destined for some governmental residence in Mexico City.

As the story went, one of the local Vera Cruz

hotel owners, a fellow named Carlos Fonseca, had a friend on the loading dock who owed him money. Shortly after their arrival, boxes containing four bathtubs were conveniently misplaced. Although the authorities investigated for several days, the boxes were nowhere to be found. Leastwise nowhere in the warehouse district. The officials, however, neglected to check Fonseca's hotel on the outskirts of town.

Fonseca might have had a chance to enjoy those tubs himself had it not been for the hotel's gaming table. Carlos liked to sit in on some of the poker games run out of his hotel's own card room. He fancied himself a sharpie, but Paco Fitzhugh was better. Fonseca, after a run of questionable bad luck, put up the tubs which were still in their shipping crates, as collateral, and promptly lost.

Rather than hanging around Vera Cruz and possibly risking unpleasant consequences, Fitzhugh wisely loaded the crates in two freight wagons and rode away the same day. It was originally his idea to head for Los Angeles, but, before hitting the border, his wagons broke down. Being more lazy than ambitious, Paco simply unloaded the tubs and set up shop. Over the years the rest of the town grew up around his bathhouse and the nearby *cantina*.

As I stretched out in a tub full of hot water, I marveled at its French craftmanship. Each of the four tubs was long enough even for someone my size to lie down in. The ends sloped gracefully upward to provide a headrest and the sides curved outwards, thick enough to serve as armrests. The bronze tub had relief work all along its edges. Dragons and knights in battle were depicted on two tubs, while Cupids, angels, and clouds highlighted the other two.

The soap was more pumice than lather, but Mario and Pablo kept a fire going out back and hot water was available at all times. Drinks were provided for a price, although it was usually three times that of the *cantina* across the way. Every customer who ever took a bath at Fitzhugh's felt like he'd died and gone to heaven, although few cowpunchers ever entered more than once. It seems most were either unwilling to meet the high price Fitzhugh charged, or preferred to spend their pay on wild women, drinks, or cards, in that order.

Over the years, most of my baths had consisted of river crossings, flash floods, or sudden rainstorms. When I was younger, though, my ma was especially particular about family cleanliness. Neither my sister nor I liked to sit still for church service, but Ma insisted we attend every Sunday. Naturally we had to clean up before, lest folks think she was raising a pack of little savages. I can still remember her bending me over a rain barrel with a washcloth in hand, exclaiming—"I knowed it! You're trying to grow apples back here!"—as she scrubbed my ears clean.

I had to fight to keep from falling asleep right there in the tub, but although I could easily have asked Mario for another tub full of hot water, I remembered that Fitzhugh charged by the hour, by the tub, and by the towel. Finally I decided enough was enough. Besides, a man shouldn't get used to too much luxury—doesn't build character, or so my cash poor friends are always quick to point out.

Standing up, I stepped out of the tub, toweled off, and dressed. As I faced the small mirror tied to the opposite wall trying to bring some sense of order to my hair, I had the uncomfortable feeling that I had forgotten something. There were serious questions that still bothered me, but try as I might, the answers eluded me.

I shrugged the feeling off at least for the moment. The next time I met Rosa I wanted to be as presentable as possible, and another glance in the mirror convinced me that a shave wouldn't hurt. I tossed a tip to the boys, hoping they'd get to keep it this time, and left in search of a barber.

The building next door to the bathhouse was a single, freestanding, converted wood frame house with a large picture window. The sign out front was written in both Spanish and English. The English part read:

> Dentist, Alchemist, and Phrenologist
> Barber extraordinaire . . . No credit!

Uncle Zeke always claimed that dentists made the best barbers. "Nobody gives as close a shave as a good dentist," he used to say. "Must be the way they're taught to sharpen instruments. Always keep a good edge on their razors." I rubbed the palm of my hand across the stubble that had formed on my face and pushed open the door.

A middle-aged man with spectacles, wearing a long white apron, was washing his hands in a sink that stood in front of a swivel-type barber chair. The room was covered with charts depicting teeth, skull configurations, and other assorted body parts.

"*¿Con permiso, está abierto?*" I asked.

He turned around and looked me over as he

finished drying his hands. Dropping the towel over the back of the chair, he finally answered. "Yep, open for business. Name's Grumet, Doctor Robert Grumet. What'll it be, gent . . . haircut, shave, or extraction?"

"Just a shave will be fine. It's that obvious I'm a *gringo*, huh?" I joked, referring to the fact that, although I'd addressed him in Spanish, he hadn't even hesitated to answer me in English.

"Over six foot tall, and with that accent? Are you kidding me?" He laughed. Dusting off the chair with the same towel, he gestured to me. "Here you go. Have a seat."

I tossed my hat on the rack near the door and settled into the chair.

With a grandiose sweep he pulled a large white sheet from the counter and spun it around my neck. Clipping it together from behind, he asked: "Want the sideburns wide, long, short, or nonexistent?"

"Clean and short will do, I guess," I answered, watching him glide his razor back and forth across the leather strop, in a timeless and traditional barbershop ceremony. *Uncle Zeke was probably right,* I thought.

"So what's a man of your obvious talents doing this far south?" I asked.

He started lathering up a small soap brush and looked down at me. "Well, I'll tell you. Ever hear of a man up Texas way named Loving? Oliver Loving?"

"Who hasn't? Drives cattle throughout the whole area. Owns most of it, too. What of it?"

"I used to practice up north. One day a drive comes through town and this cowboy drops in complaining of a sore tooth. At least I thought he was a cowpoke. With all that dust and dirt it was hard to tell the steers from the ramrods. This fellow had a badly infected back molar . . . you know the kind, a real challenge."

I grimaced and nodded. He was still lathering the brush so I leaned back and tried to relax.

"Anyway, I was anxious to try out this new elixir I'd bought from this traveling supplier, name of Moser, Conrad Moser. Ever heard of him?"

"Nope," I replied.

"Well, sir, this elixir was supposed to kill pain better than a jug of straight Tennessee moonshine. It didn't come with no instructions, so I told the cowpoke to drink about half the bottle. Figured that ought to do the trick. Sure enough, he passed right out and I started chiseling away. That tooth was real impacted so it took a little longer than I thought it would. Guess I didn't notice how long the patient sat there without moving. When I finished pulling the tooth and straightened up, I noticed he was sort of blue. I slapped his face a little, but he just sat there with his mouth open, staring off into space." Dr. Grumet shook his head in thought, and then started to soap up my beard with the brush. "Yep, that fellow just sat there . . . all paralyzed, eyes open, and staring off into space. Couldn't get his mouth to close, neither. I pricked him a couple of times to test him, but he weren't moving. I swear I thought he was dead. Just then the door opened and another cowboy stuck his head in and asked if Mister Loving was finished yet. Not quite, I says. I had him covered over with my drape so's the other couldn't see, but, as he turns to leave, he says he hopes things work out all right 'cause they'd hung the last dentist what hurt the boss. Well, I'll tell you, I packed up my bags, locked the door, and hightailed it right out of there. Didn't stop till I crossed the border, either."

"You kill him or not?" I asked.

"No, sir. It turns out Mister Loving survived, after all. But he must have woke up awfully mad. Guess that was all the screaming I heard when I lit a shuck out of town. Luckily things worked out for me in the end. I got a nice little practice here and don't plan on going back."

As he took the straight razor in hand, I sat upright in the chair silently praying that he was more proficient at shaving. Fortunately it turned out to be a needless worry as he skillfully ran the razor back and forth, without even a nick.

"Let me ask you a question," I said, noticeably relieved. "You deal a lot with the public around here. Ever see a tall, heavy-set cowboy, about my size, similar color hair, with thick eyebrows and a thin moustache? Had a healed-up broke nose and a cleft chin. Wore his pistols cross-draw, butts forward. Maybe a couple of months back?"

"Not in here, but it seems like I do remember someone like that walking past my window on a few occasions. Noticed him 'cause of them double pistols you mentioned. Most folks around here can hardly afford even one." He eyed the ivory grip on my Navy Colt. "Friend o' yours?"

"Not hardly," I answered. "You said he walked by a few times. Headed anywhere in particular?"

"Ain't much else down this way exceptin' the fruit market and the telegraph office. He didn't strike me as the type to be shopping for apples." Dr. Grumet looked down again at my Colt. "Ain't gonna ask why you're so curious. I've had enough problems for one lifetime, thank you."

So I was right. Luke Pierce had come to San Rafael to recruit men and to keep Davies informed by telegraph. Still, one thing bothered me. There was no way that Pierce could have known beforehand that we would change directions once the drive began. I hadn't discussed my plans with anyone until the very morning that I explained it to *Don* Enrique and his *caporal*.

Pierce and his bunch might simply have trailed the herd from a distance, but I had been far out in front when I was shot. So how could Pierce have possibly gotten into position to dry-gulch me, unless he knew well ahead of time where I was going? But how could he know that?

According to Chavez, no one left camp that day and nobody reëntered camp until the attack. There was no telegraph on the trail, and, if anything were being left behind as a signal, the drag riders would have noticed and they were rotated too often to be suspect themselves.

As I sat there thinking, the glare of reflected sunlight off his mirror hit me squarely in the eyes, causing me to squint in pain. Dr. Grumet almost drew blood when I jerked my head.

"Sorry about that, mister. Sun always does that around this time of day. Been meaning to put some curtains on that window. Here let me fix it." He adjusted a knob on the side of the chair and began to swivel it in an attempt to avoid the glare. As the chair moved back and forth in front of his mirror, the sunbeam kept reflecting on and off into my eyes. I suddenly knew! Planting my feet on the ground to stop the chair, I jumped up and pulled the sheet from my neck, using it to wipe the lather off.

"Something the matter?" he asked.

"It's OK, Doc, I just remembered something important." I tossed him a few coins. "You've been a great help. Nice close shave, too," I added.

"Sure you won't let me check that mouth for you?" he asked.

My jaw clamped down instinctively and I flinched a little. "No thanks, maybe some other time."

Chapter Twenty-four

Later that afternoon Rosa, Chavez, Sonora, and I were waiting next to her buckboard when Miguel emerged from the livery, leading his horse.

"*¡Oye,* Miguel, *ven acá!*" I shouted, calling him over.

He tied his horse to the nearest hitch and crossed the street to join us.

"What's up?" he asked, smiling.

Rosa was the first to answer him. "My father is riding to town to join us, but he is a little overdue. Would you please ride up into the hills outside of town and watch for him?"

"*Sí, Señorita* Rosa, I'll leave right away," he replied, turning toward his horse.

Chavez stopped him with a hand on his shoulder. "Perhaps it would be a good idea to signal us when he is in sight. But . . . ," he hesitated, "it will be too far for us to hear you shout and a rifle shot might give the *don* the wrong idea. What do you think, *gringo?*"

"You're right," I answered. "After all that he's been through, the last thing ***Don*** Enrique would want to hear is more rifle fire." I paused a moment as if deep in thought.

"Wait a minute, I've got an idea," Sonora

chipped in, right on cue. "How about usin' a mirror?"

"That's a good idea," Rosa agreed. "There may be one here in my wagon."

I rummaged around in the back of the buckboard and pulled out a small piece of mirror that we had planted there earlier. I tossed it over to Miguel. "Here, you can use this to signal us with."

"*Andale,* Miguel, before it gets too dark," said Chavez.

It had all happened so quickly Miguel didn't have time to think things out. He just nodded to us and hurried back to his horse. Just before he reached it, however, I called out to him again.

"*Oye,* Miguel, *un momento.* One more thing."

He turned around again. "What is it?"

"You sure you know how to send mirror signs?"

"*Por supuesto* . . . of course, my father taught me. Many in our village use mirrors that way."

"That how you let the Four Box brand know where our herd was goin'? Is that how you sent them after me, *amigo?*" I stared him right in the eye, and stepped away from the rest, facing him in the middle of the street.

Miguel looked around desperately, but had no cover nearby.

Rosa moved out of the way, back behind her buckboard, while Chavez and the other ***vaqueros*** on both sides of the street moved to block his escape.

"I never could understand how those rustlers managed to anticipate all our moves without a mistake, and without us knowing," I said.

"You see, Miguel, they knew Chavez and I always double checked our back trail. They had to stay far enough away so that we'd never pick up their tracks. Hard to follow if you're that far back. But then they could do it easily enough if they already knew ahead of time where we were going, couldn't they? A mirror shines light for miles, doesn't it, Miguel?"

"*¿Como?* You are wrong. It was not me," he answered nervously.

In the corner of my eye I noticed Pili standing behind the *cantina* doors. Several of the townspeople were lined up along the walk watching us, but none seemed threatening.

"Had to be you, *chico*. Luke Pierce used the town telegraph before we left town. So he already knew all about the drive. Francisco and you were the only ones in town after the drive was planned. Remember, that's how we met. But you see, the *caporal* and I already know Francisco can't read mirror sign. . . ."

Miguel's gun hand dropped slowly to his side.

"Always seemed to me you spent just a little too much time shaving in the morning. I understand now. Good opportunity to use your mirror. I'll bet Joaquin wouldn't have appreciated your generous offers to help him shine his pots so much had he known you were also using them to signal with. It got him killed, didn't it?" I started walking slowly toward him, my right hand down at my side.

"Miguel, you betrayed us just for money?" Francisco shouted from across the street. "Why? Didn't *Don* Enrique treat us fairly?"

"This is between us two. Stay out of it, Cisco!" I yelled, without once taking my eyes off Miguel.

"You sent them after me, Miguel, didn't you? Had them bushwhack me from hiding. Why'd you do it? *¿Porqué?*"

"A man needs enough money for his own place. I would never be good enough just working for others." As he answered, I caught him releasing his holster thong.

"Who gave you that idea, Miguel?" I asked. "Never be good enough for who?"

He never gave me time to find out. Instead, he dropped quickly to one knee, drew, and fired. He was very fast, and the sudden move might have worked had he only waited a touch longer and not jerked his shot so much.

Pa's words echoed in my ears. "Shootin' first don't always cut it. Ya got to hit what you aim at, too. And, Son, don't trust to one shot, either, you keep shootin' until the threat is over. Remember, boy, only a fool stands still in a gunfight."

Miguel had aimed too quickly, firing at the very spot where I had been standing only an instant before. I side-stepped to my left just as he dropped, causing him to lose whatever edge he might have hoped for. My first shot didn't miss him, though, nor did the next three. Miguel died in the middle of that street, curled into a lifeless ball.

Although I got no satisfaction from what had just happened, there was no remorse this time. It was his call, not mine, and he, like others in the past, had gotten what he deserved.

I holstered the Colt, suddenly feeling very weary, but relieved that the ordeal was finally over. I had fulfilled my promise to Rosa María, and could now begin seriously to consider the possibility of building a future with someone I cared deeply for. I felt a warm sense of well-being come over me, and was anxious to be with her forever.

Looking off to my left, I saw Rosa standing in her buckboard, facing me with a rifle in her arms. The next thing I knew, something struck me and I was flung forward into the dirt. There was a sharp pain in my chest and I had trouble breathing. Everything seemed to be spinning. I looked up and gasped.

"Rosa. What . . . ?"

The last thing I remember before passing out was seeing her lever another round as she raised the rifle up to her shoulder.

I was content to lie where I was, warm and comfortable. But before long, I began to wonder just exactly where that was. I could detect a faint smell of perfume in the air and heard soft voices nearby that I couldn't quite identify. It was clear I wasn't still face down in the street, but, since I didn't have the strength to sit up, I was forced to lie there, confused. I drifted in and out of sleep. The whole time my body rested, my mind fought for answers.

Over time it slowly came back to me, Miguel, the shoot-out, everything. The sudden realization that I'd been shot caused me to bolt upright. My eyes opened wide but captured nothing but pitch black darkness. My arms stretched out to feel but I couldn't reach anything, either. I tried to make out where the voices were coming from, what they were saying, or who they belonged to, but couldn't hear anything clearly enough to be of help.

I fell backward and started sweating profusely. When I tried to roll over, a sharp stabbing pain almost crushed the air from my lungs. I collapsed onto my back, exhausted.

"Where am I? Who's there?" I tried to yell, but my voice was hoarse and distant, almost unrecognizable. I was so disoriented, I couldn't even be sure if I was really making any sound.

A door finally opened to my right and light filtered in. A figure moved toward me and then paused. A match was struck and a lamp was lit. The glow hurt my eyes, causing me to swing an arm up over my face.

"Relax. You're back at our *hacienda*. You're safe." It sounded like Rosa's voice, although right then and there it wouldn't have been too hard to convince me the words had come from an angel. She took a wet towel from a pan on the table next to the bed, bent over, and wiped my forehead.

"Why, Rosa? What . . . ?"

"Pilar shot you from the *cantina*. *¡Desgraciada!* She always was looking for someone rich to take her away from here. Pilar must have promised to go with Miguel if only he got enough money."

"I don't understand."

"Miguel was desperately in love with her and would have done anything she wanted. Pilar must have convinced him to betray us for money. She never was satisfied, that one, always looking for the easy life. Pilar would stop at nothing to get out of this pueblo, even if she had to make a fool of an innocent *vaquero*, or shoot a man in the back. Poor Miguel never had a chance with a she-devil like her."

"You're probably right about that," I said.

Pierce must have recruited her first, and Pilar, in turn, corrupted Miguel over to their side. She must have been the girl who arranged to have the telegraph messages sent to Davies. Miguel would have helped her translate them. What a web! "So, what finally happened to her?" I asked. "Where's Pili now?"

"Where she belongs," replied Rosa.

I suddenly recalled watching Rosa swing her rifle in my direction. She must have fired directly across me. "You shot her?" I asked.

She nodded. "She got what she deserved. I did what I had to. Besides," Rosa said, looking down into my eyes with a smile, "I couldn't very well let her kill a man who was about to ask me to marry him, could I?"

"I was?" I stammered, taken completely off guard.

She just looked down at me, hard, and frowned.

"I mean, I am!" I said a little more convincingly.

She smiled, bent down, and kissed me softly.

"Duermate, mi amor. Sleep." Rosa blew out the lamp and left the room, closing the door quietly after her.

My Navy Colt and holster hung from the bedpost, with my Henry rifle propped up in the far corner. The room was peaceful and quiet, and that night I went to sleep one painful but very contented *hombre*.

ABOUT THE AUTHOR

R. W. Stone inherited his love for Western adventure from his father, a former Army Air Corps armaments officer and horse enthusiast. He taught his son both to ride and shoot at a very early age. Many of those who grew up in the late 1950s and early 1960s remember it as a time before urban sprawl when Western adventure predominated both television and the cinema, and Stone began writing later in life in an attempt to recapture some of that past spirit he had enjoyed as a youth. In 1974 Stone graduated from the University of Illinois with honors in Animal Science. After living in Mexico for five years, he later graduated from the National Autonomous University's College of Veterinary Medicine and moved to Florida. Over the years he has served as President of the South Florida Veterinary Medical Association, the Lake County Veterinary Medical Association, and as executive secretary for three national veterinary organizations. Dr. Stone is currently the Chief of Staff of the Veterinary Trauma Center of Groveland, an advanced level care facility. He is the author of over seventy scientific articles and has lectured internationally. Still a firearms collector, horse enthusiast, and now a black-belt-ranked martial artist, R.W.

Stone presently lives in Central Florida with his wife, two daughters, one horse, and three dogs. He is presently working on his next western, *Vengeance Is Mine*.

LOUIS L'AMOUR

Grub Line Rider

Louis L'Amour is one of the most popular and honored authors of the past hundred years. Millions of readers have thrilled to his tales of courage and adventure, tales that have transported them to the Old West and brought to life that exciting era of American history. Here, collected together in paperback for the first time, are seven of L'Amour's finest stories, all carefully restored to their original magazine publication versions.

Whether he's writing about a cattle town in Montana ("Black Rock Coffin Makers"), a posse pursuit across the desert ("Desert Death Song"), a young gunfighter ("Ride, You Tonto Riders"), or a violent battle to defend a homestead ("Grub Line Rider"), L'Amour's powerful presentation of the American West is always vibrant and compelling. This volume represents a golden opportunity to experience these stories as Louis L'Amour originally intended them to be read.

ISBN 13: 978-0-8439-6065-5

MAX BRAND®

Luck

Pierre Ryder is not your average Jesuit missionary. He's able to ride the meanest horse, run for miles without tiring, and put a bullet in just about any target. But now he's on a mission of vengeance to find the man who killed his father. The journey will test his endurance to its utmost—and so will the extraordinary woman he meets along the way. Jacqueline "Jack" Boone has all the curves of a lady but can shoot better than most men. In the epic tradition of *Riders of the Purple Sage*, their story is one for the ages.

ISBN 13: 978-0-8439-5875-1
